Midas's Bride

MYRNA MACKENZIE

SILHOUETTE Romance®

Published by Silhouette Books

America's Publisher of Contemporary Romance

SILHOUETTE BOOKS

ISBN 0-373-19719-5

MIDAS'S BRIDE

This edition published by arrangement with Harlequin Books S.A.

Visit Silhouette Books at www.eHarlequin.com

Printed in U.S.A.

Books by Myrna Mackenzie

Silhouette Romance

The Baby Wish #1046
The Daddy List #1090
Babies and a Blue-Eyed Man #1182
The Secret Groom #1225
The Scandalous Return of Jake Walker #1256
Prince Charming's Return #1361
**Simon Says... Marry Me!* #1429
**At the Billionaire's Bidding* #1442
**Contractually His* #1454
The Billionaire Is Back #1520
Blind-Date Bride #1526
A Very Special Delivery #1540
**Bought by the Billionaire* #1610
**The Billionaire's Bargain* #1622
**The Billionaire Borrows a Bride* #1634
†*The Pied Piper's Bride* #1714
†*Midas's Bride* #1719

*The Wedding Auction
†The Brides of Red Rose

Silhouette Books

Montana Mavericks
Just Pretending

Lone Star Country Club
Her Sweet Talkin' Man

Family Secrets
Blind Attraction

MYRNA MACKENZIE,

winner of the Holt Medallion honoring outstanding literary talent, believes that there are many unsung heroes and heroines living among us, and she loves to write about such people. She tries to inject her characters with humor, loyalty and honor, and after many years of writing she is still thrilled to be able to say that she makes her living by daydreaming. Myrna lives with her husband and two sons in the suburbs of Chicago. During the summer she likes to take long walks, and during cold Chicago winters, she likes to *think* about taking long walks (or dream of summers in Maine). Readers may write to Myrna at P.O. Box 225, LaGrange, IL 60525, or they may visit her online at www.myrnamackenzie.com.

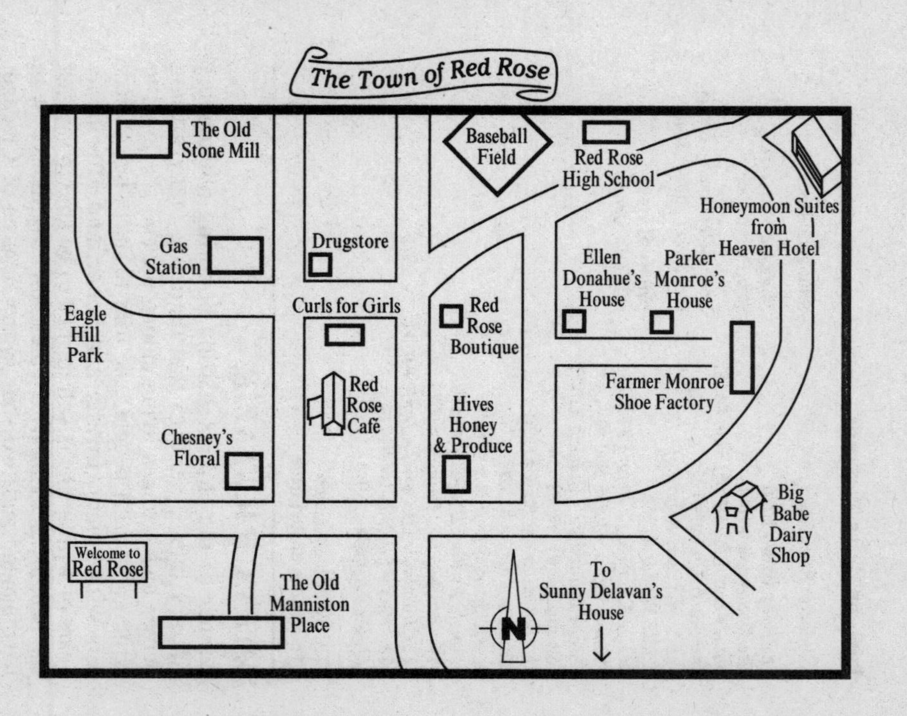
The Town of Red Rose
The Old Stone Mill
Gas Station
Drugstore
Baseball Field
Red Rose High School
Honeymoon Suites from Heaven Hotel
Ellen Donahue's House
Parker Monroe's House
Curls for Girls
Red Rose Boutique
Eagle Hill Park
Red Rose Café
Farmer Monroe Shoe Factory
Hives Honey & Produce
Chesney's Floral
Big Babe Dairy Shop
Welcome to Red Rose
The Old Manniston Place
N
To Sunny Delavan's House

Chapter One

A haven. That was what this place was, Abigail Chesney thought as she drained her third cup of decaf and let the friendly chatter of the women at the Red Rose Café flow around her. Here she could temporarily escape her problems. She was safe.

"The problem is, we may have had a few men moving to Red Rose in the past couple of weeks, but we're still overflowing with women," Lydia Eunique, the sixtyish, silver-haired mayor and owner of the Red Rose said. "The town still needs men, and lots of them."

Delia Sable, a young, blue-eyed blonde who worked for Abigail at Chesney's Floral, glanced briefly at her boss, her gaze slipping to Abby's abdomen before she hastily looked away. Abby almost wanted to laugh. Had she really thought that the Red Rose was safe? Heck, this was small-town Illinois. Everyone knew her business and her concerns.

There was no escaping her condition. Out of deference to friendship, no one would mention the fact that she was four months pregnant and unmarried, but they knew, and they also knew that of all of them, she was most in need of a man fast even if she didn't want one. Safe? Well, safe had never been a word she had bothered with in her life. Why start now?

"We don't want just any men," she said, setting her coffee cup down.

"That's true," Joyce Hives, the owner of Hive's Honey and Produce said, nodding, her light-brown braid bobbing along. "We want men who'll make good fathers and husbands and lovers."

Not good lovers. Abby had to swallow hard to keep the words from erupting from her mouth. Not good-looking drifters, not men who thought they were looking for love, not men who wanted real relationships. Just the basics, just good father material. But then that was just her. She couldn't speak for the rest of her friends.

"Well, maybe that's what we're getting," Sunny Delavan, a big, well-proportioned woman who owned the Big Babe Dairy Shop said. "Since Ellie talked Parker Monroe into coming back to town, there's been a trickle of men following him. And most of them are good." Sunny grumbled a bit as she said this. One of Parker's friends, Chester, had a thing for Sunny, and for some reason, Sunny, who loved most men, didn't want to give Chester the time of day. Probably because Chester saw right through her tough act to the soft woman inside. "Maybe in time we'll all find what we want."

"I just hope it's sooner rather than later," Rosellen January said, shifting her tall, narrow frame in her chair.

Abby was sure that the comment was made in reference to her own condition, even though everyone was trying hard not to look at her and make her feel more self-conscious than she already was. Maybe it was time to stop drinking coffee and get back to work. While Delia minded the shop, Abby and a small crew tended the landscaping side of the business in the surrounding area, and in the summer there was plenty to do. Besides, this talk was making her and everyone else uncomfortable. She should just go quietly, and ratchet down the stress factor that was rising in the Red Rose.

"We can't rush things and risk doing something stupid. The baby's going to be born whether there's a father for it or not," she said, glancing over the rim of her coffee cup. And there definitely wasn't a father. Dennis, who had lived two towns over, had headed for Alaska as soon as he'd gotten wind of the baby brewing inside Abby. It wasn't the first time a Chesney woman had been left high and dry by a man.

And Dennis's hasty retreat was no secret. For a while Lydia had posted a dart board with Dennis's face on it, until Abby took it down. The darn thing was too big a reminder of her own idiocy in believing the engagement ring Dennis had placed on her finger meant that he really wanted her and all that she stood for.

In truth, he probably never really had wanted her. He'd had trouble dealing with her blatant independent streak from the first and had viewed her as a physical challenge, but Dennis had known all the right words, and she'd had a weak moment. Who would have thought she could have gotten pregnant after just one slip-up? Certainly not Dennis, it seemed. Anyway, he was gone, thank goodness, and she was smarter now, and much more realistic. Her baby might only have her to care for it, and if that happened she would handle it.

"That's all there is to it," she said. "Let's just face

the fact that I'm unmarried and pregnant, and there isn't any daddy in sight.''

''Abby, that's okay. You know we're all going to be here for you and the little one,'' Sunny said. ''But there's more to it than that. Dennis might have been the world's biggest jerk, but you can't paint all the men in the world with the brush meant for him. You do want a father for your baby, hon,'' Sunny said. ''We all know that.''

Yes, they did know that, because every last one of them was aware that her father had left before she had been born and that she wanted something for her baby that she hadn't had.

''Maybe so, but do I look worried, Sunny? I'm a big girl. I like challenges, and besides, we don't always get what we want. Sometimes that's a blessing, especially where Dennis was concerned,'' she said with a wide smile that didn't exactly work. No matter, she'd spent her whole life brazening through. People here expected it of her and didn't fault her for it.

''We'd still like you to have a good, honest, steadfast man,'' Lydia said.

''For the baby,'' Abby said slowly. ''Not for me.'' She was adamant about that. Everyone knew that. She'd told them before that that wasn't what she wanted. ''No dynamics, no good looks, doesn't have to be a genius and definitely shouldn't be strong willed. I think one in a family is enough. Just a good, simple, kind man who wants a child and won't mind having a wife to boot. But that's no problem. I'm on it. I've already talked to Thomasina, and we're going to take our time about finding a good fit, so I want you all to stop worrying.''

For several seconds after she uttered the name of the local matchmaker, there was dead silence in the room.

Probably it was partly because in the past few lean years they'd all considered going to the matchmaker once or twice themselves. But just as much of the strained silence was due to the fact that none of them really had any faith in Thomasina's abilities to come up with the right man. Thomasina herself was still single at age thirty-nine, and with the dearth of men the last few years, even the overly optimistic matchmaker had given up trying to fix people up. She'd only ventured back into business a few days ago, and no woman at the Red Rose had signed on. The general consensus was that a woman who couldn't find her own man wasn't likely to find one for another woman.

"Oh. Thomasina. That's good," Delia finally said, and Abby almost thought Delia was going to pat her hand the way one would pat a small child to make them feel better. "But if by some chance Thomasina doesn't manage to find someone, maybe the new businesses that Parker and Ellie are bringing to town will sweep someone along who'll suit. You know we love you, Abby. And I do wish you'd find someone handsome and charming and passionate and…oh…just perfect!"

Abby closed her eyes to keep from shaking Delia. The young woman always had a dreamy look in her eyes. She created amazingly wonderful flower arrangements for Abby's shop and she was patient and helpful with the customers, but Delia was a romantic through and through. There was no way she could understand just how panicky her words made Abby feel. Abby and her mother before her might have had green thumbs, but where men were concerned, everything they touched turned brown and died. Suddenly Abby needed air. She had to get out of here.

With a clunk, Abby set her coffee down and rose,

ordering herself to appear calm as she smiled and turned to everyone. "You all have a great day," she heard herself say, her tone excessively cheery. "I'd like to stay, but, oh man, I've got just tons and tons of plants to tend."

And a future it was impossible to run from, she thought, forcing herself to resist smoothing her hand over her abdomen.

A chorus of goodbyes met her, and Abby turned toward the door just as it opened wide.

A tall, dark-haired man stepped inside, his broad shoulders just clearing the doorway. He glanced around the room, his lazy, sexy, silver eyes taking in the room filled with women.

"I hope I'm not intruding," he said slowly. "But I was told that I might find Abigail Chesney here."

All her friends turned toward her. And then the man in the doorway focused those gorgeous silver eyes on her. His look was so intent, it singled her out from the crowd so completely that Abby almost took a step back.

She didn't. She wouldn't. No one, especially not he, was going to see that she could be even a tiny bit affected by a man giving her the once-over, particularly a man who was a total stranger. She just wasn't going to be a weakling idiot again. The Chesney women might have a penchant for cluelessness in choosing men, but they were also fast learners who didn't keep repeating their mistakes.

Abby raised her chin. "It seems you've found your target. How can I help you?" And how can I manage to move this conversation to someplace less public? she wondered. She knew that Delia, at the very least, would be spinning some romantic nonsense about this man.

"I have a job I'd like to commission you for. I've heard that you're the best in the area."

She almost managed to smile at that one. "I'm the only."

He grinned. "Then you're definitely the best."

Someone giggled, but Abby didn't allow herself to smile. "What kind of job would that be?" she asked. She really should move this conversation outside. She wanted to, except then it would be just him and her without the barrier of her friends.

"A big one. A very big one. My name is Griffin O'Dell. I just bought—"

"The old Manniston place," she finished for him. She knew that. It had been a favorite haunt when she was a child. She'd never met Griffin O'Dell, but it was clear from the looks on some of the women's faces that they had. He was a college friend of Parker Monroe's, and Parker had grown up in Red Rose, had recently returned and was now going to marry Ellie Donahue.

At Parker's behest, Griffin had come here once before for just a day or two, a couple of weeks earlier when Parker had staged a town open house to attract business and the men that the women had requested. Mr. O'Dell's visit hadn't been long at all, but he'd had time enough to buy the huge property just outside of town. And obviously he'd had enough time to get a number of the women here swooning and glowing. "What is it you want to do with your land?" she managed to say.

"Transform it into sports fields. Lots of them. I'm in the sporting goods business, but I'll be here for the summers when my son comes to visit me. I bought my land here, because I want him to have the kind of place little boys dream of, room to run with lots of open spaces and fresh air. But I can't stop working for the whole summer. I also need a unique forum to showcase my products to clients I'll invite here. It's a bit of a rush job, I'm afraid. I've already invited my first business associates here. They'll arrive in a month."

He'd be here just for the summers? Ah, a drifter of sorts. She knew the type all too well, although this one was wealthier than the ones she'd met. More handsome and compelling, too, she thought, before she caught herself. What the heck was she doing even speculating about this man? She knew nothing of him, hadn't even laid eyes on him before two minutes ago. And what was that he'd said about sports fields?

"I'm sorry," she said with what might have been too much enthusiasm, "but I'm afraid I can't help you. I don't know a thing about building sports fields."

He shook his head and smiled. She thought she heard the women behind her sighing, and she flinched, wishing she could tell them to hush. A man like this didn't need any encouragement. He probably had women dropping their hankies in front of him all the time and didn't need to let his head get any bigger.

"You don't need to know any of that. That's not your part," he said softly, and it sounded like he was talking about something other than business.

She swallowed with difficulty. "I don't understand." Somehow she managed to get an edge into her voice, even though with him staring at her, she felt dreadfully aware of her body beneath her loose sleeveless white shirt and jeans.

"Then I'll help you," he said. "The land has been lying unused for so long that it's overgrown and unkempt. It needs landscaping, something that will set the house off and that will provide a buffer between my property and the next one. I'd like to have an area for my son and my guests to wander. My land is spacious and it suits my business purposes, but it needs some beauty. I need you to do that for me,'' he said, and this time Abby couldn't swallow.

All she had to do was say no, but the word stuck in her mind. What reason could she give for turning down this job? Big jobs didn't come her way in Red Rose. All her friends knew that. Arguing that she couldn't work with a man whose very voice made her shiver and whose eyes made her insides turn to warm liquid was just the kind of thing she would never admit. It implied weakness, and she wouldn't be weak ever again. At least not about a man.

Instead she nodded. ''I'll have to look over the situation.''

''I'll drive you,'' Griffin O'Dell said, and he held out his hand. ''Would right now be too soon?''

She didn't close her eyes the way she wanted to. She didn't say, Yes, anytime in the next lifetime would be too soon. She didn't say, I'm afraid to touch you for fear that I'm going to either faint or feel some erotic sensation I definitely do *not* want to feel.

She folded her arms and shook her head. ''Right now will be fine.''

Safe. What in the world had she been thinking? The Red Rose Café had just turned into the most unsafe place in the world.

Thank goodness she had plans with Thomasina. Her trip to the matchmaker had been the source of her concern only minutes ago. Now she could see that it was going to be her salvation.

Griffin drew Abigail Chesney out to his car, the tension in her arm evident the whole way, though she followed him easily enough. For some reason, this woman did not like him. Or at least she didn't want to go with him, and he had a good feeling that she didn't even want the work he was offering her. And yet...

He looked down at her as they neared his car. "You know the Manniston place then," he said, helping her inside his black Jaguar.

"It's a favorite of mine," she answered when he had taken his seat beside her. "I love the charm of old familiar places." She stared pointedly at him.

Ouch. He smiled. "Don't worry, so do I, Ms. Chesney. I'm not going to hurt an old friend."

Those wide blue eyes didn't even blink. "It's your property, Mr. O'Dell." But that stare was so pointed, her soft voice so cool that it was clear that she didn't like the fact that he had bought the place.

Too bad. He needed a place to bring Casey. He was desperate for some alone time with his son, and he had to have some way to counteract his ex-wife's attempts to discredit him as a father because he traveled so much and supposedly couldn't provide the necessary stability. In the year since the divorce had become final, Cheryl had done her best to take as much of Casey's time as she could, and if she found a way, she would take the little that Griffin still held on to.

Well, that wasn't going to happen. Red Rose was a small, stable town, he had a good friend here in Parker and Casey adored Parker. What's more, the Manniston place was a heck of a great house and the grounds were made for a four-year-old boy moving into his growing up years. He planned to firmly plant himself here for the duration of the summers he was allotted with his child, and if Abigail Chesney with her wayward strawberry curls and her who-the-hell-are-you? expression didn't like him being there, he couldn't do anything about that.

"It's my property," he agreed, finally addressing her comment. "My little boy will be here very shortly. I want this to be a home away from home for him."

Ah, she had a heart after all. Her dark lashes fluttered down for a second, she twisted her hands in her lap before she looked at him again. "My apologies. I was out of line," she said.

He shook his head as he eased the car down the road. "I'm the newcomer here, and a temporary one at best. It's only to be expected that people will resent me coming in to change things."

"No. That's not right. We've courted change of late. If I have nostalgic memories of your home, it's because the Mannistons left it deserted, and I liked the joys of trespassing in a place I had no business being in the first place. It was theirs then, and it's yours now. I borrowed the memories, but they were free and they're mine to keep. I won't be snooty about you making changes. I really have no interest in your home."

"Except for the grounds," he reminded her.

"I haven't agreed to do that yet. We might not see eye to eye on things. I have a tendency to be a bit pigheaded about my business, and I don't compromise for things I consider silly."

He chuckled. "Like building a lot of sports fields on a long, lovely expanse of lawn?"

She turned slightly pink, a very pretty shade of pink. He had the feeling that she didn't like the fact that she was a blusher, since she immediately turned her head to stare out the side window. Abigail Chesney was clearly a very proud woman.

"We'll see," she said.

He stopped the car and pulled to the side just before the entrance to his property. "It's not a negotiable issue, Ms. Chesney. The sports fields are business, and I can't give up a whole summer to play, even though I love my son to death. If I can't be at my normal place of work, I intend to bring that work here.

"Your friend, Ellie Donahue, helped me form this idea, and it's a good one, a unique one. O'Dell Hall will have a demonstration area for as many sports as possible, I'll bring my newest and finest products here, and then I'll invite my most promising clients to visit. They'll be wined and dined, they'll get a chance to try out my top-of-the-line products firsthand in a social atmosphere, and I'll treat them to the hospitality of your lovely town. You see, I'm very serious about my work, Abby. It's what makes me tick. It's all I have when Casey isn't around. So I'm counting on you to make an unconventional use of space surrounding a house look right. I've been told you're a wizard with plants."

She turned at that and blinked, and those blue eyes looked suddenly vulnerable. He would just bet she'd hate that.

"What else have you been told?" she asked, and he noticed that one hand curved gently over her abdomen. It was a gesture Cheryl had often used when she was carrying Casey. Otherwise he would never have noted it. He also noted the lack of a ring on her finger.

Chances were he was wrong about jumping to conclusions about the pregnancy. She was slender and unmarried, lovely and slightly hostile. He was out of sorts with the types of compromises he was having to make to gain access to his child when he should have had the right to see Casey whenever he pleased. Perhaps he wasn't seeing things exactly straight. After all, it was a woman who had brought him to this desperate phase of his life, and there was a good chance he was taking out his frustration with Cheryl on Abigail by jumping to all the wrong conclusions about her. Still, as he stared at her hand over her abdomen, she colored up completely again and yanked her hand away.

Griffin raised a brow. Interesting. The lovely red-haired landscaper was turning out to be more complicated than he had expected. This was supposed to be a simple job—a big job, but one that shouldn't have posed any challenges.

And it wasn't going to. If the lady wouldn't do what he wanted, he'd look farther afield. The next town or the one after that. Money talked, as he'd learned early in life, and he had plenty of money. Making it was his gift; he had the touch. What he'd never had was the right way with women, but he didn't want to waste time looking for a new landscaper when he had one here right beside him.

"What else have I been told?" he finally said. "Not much, which is fine. I like to make up my own mind about things," he said, as he threw the car into gear and cruised down the drive, stopping on the gravel pad. He palmed the keys, exited the car and circled round to help Abigail out. "Here it is," he said, gesturing with a wide sweep of his arm. "Your palette."

Ah, a smile at last. She opened her mouth to say something. He held up one hand.

"I know. You haven't said you'll take the job yet. What can I do to convince you?"

She tipped her head back and gazed up at him, and he realized that she was almost a full head shorter than he. But there wasn't an ounce of back-down in her stance. Right now she held a fair share of the cards, or at least she thought she did. Or maybe she really just didn't care about him and his job, which was probably more to the point. It was a novel situation. He didn't handle women well, but they'd always seemed to want him. Here was one who clearly didn't.

"What can you do to convince me? Give me free rein," she said, her voice firm and husky. It was a sexy voice. He'd bet it would be a huge mistake to ever tell her that.

"Free rein? Can't do. I need to approve."

She tucked her chin in stubbornly. "All right, promise me you'll protect what I plant."

He smiled. "That I can do. No one understands the pride of a person's work better than I do, Ms. Chesney. Your art will be sacred."

She made a face. "I'm a lot less formal than that. Just don't let any big football player types trample my stuff." There was a trace of bewilderment in her voice.

"Known a few insensitive males in your time?"

She froze. Her hand curved over her abdomen once again. Bad move, O'Dell, he thought. "Forget I said that. I know business, but I'm not much good with more sensitive relationships. Pretty much sworn off anything that involves things that are more complicated than contracts and dollars."

And to his amazement, she relaxed. She chuckled. "Mr. O'Dell, that was the absolute right thing to say. I'm not much good with sensitive relationships, either. Terrible, in fact. And I'm with you on the contracts and dollars all the way. I think maybe you and I might be able to do business. You need a good place for your son? Well, I have a few things I need to take care of myself, and a job this size will allow me to do that."

He studied her intently. "That's interesting. I could have sworn you didn't want this job at all."

"I don't, for a number of reasons I'd rather not get into. But as much as I'd like to say no on a gut level, my head is still working just fine, and it says be sensible, Abby."

"You have lots of conversations with yourself?"

She shrugged. "We all have our faults, Mr. O'Dell."

"Faults can be interesting."

She didn't answer. He figured he'd overstepped a boundary into the personal again. Ah well, he was, as he'd said, best at business, anyway. "You'll turn my grounds into something out of the ordinary?" he asked.

"I'll give you paradise," she promised, and she held out her hand and smiled up into his eyes.

A promise of paradise? From a woman whose voice belonged in a boudoir or a bordello, or simply in a man's bed? For a second Griffin hesitated. He took the time to remind himself that women were off his list, other than for business or for the most basic kind of pleasure. He had never been able to give women what they wanted, dating all the way back to that time when his mother's best friend had come on to him. It was a habit he'd carried into his marriage, and so, no, he didn't get involved. Relationships were too risky, too potentially painful—and not just for him. He had Casey to worry about, and from here on out everything was either Casey or work. Period. But as he took Abigail's hand, her skin smooth against his, he allowed himself to savor the soft sensation of woman. Just for a second. He noted how glistening and plump her lips were. He wondered how she would kiss. An innocent brush of her mouth or something more lush? Interesting question.

And he figured that if he ever attempted to find out the answer, he would soon be remembering what it felt like to have a black eye, something he hadn't experienced in a good many years.

Griffin grinned. The pain just might be worth it. Once, anyway. "Let's do business, Ms. Chesney. Call me Griff or Griffin."

She nodded. "I'm Abby." And when she looked up at him this time, her eyes were clear. Those lips smiled back at him again. "Show me everything."

Chapter Two

Pick up the phone and make the call, Abby told herself the next morning, but her hand hovered over the receiver, and she just couldn't do it. The fact was that what she'd told her friends at the diner wasn't exactly right. She *had* talked to Thomasina in a general way, but she still hadn't committed to letting the matchmaker find her a husband.

She wanted a father for her baby. She really did. It wasn't that she needed a man. Not at all. She was one of the most self-sufficient women she knew. It was just that she wanted her child to have what she'd never had.

Abby sighed and backed away from the telephone. It was all well and good to have noble thoughts about finding a father for her baby, but the truth was that she really wasn't sure what to do about the man's relationship with her. There wasn't a chance that she wanted what most women did, and how did you ask a man for simple friendship and family and still insist on giving nothing more? Besides, there was something so demeaning about asking someone to help her find a husband.

She just couldn't do it. Yet.

The whole helplessness of the situation infuriated her, and so as she dressed to head over to Griffin's place, Abby was in a heck of a snit.

She snatched up the tentative drawings he'd faxed to her and headed out to her baby-blue pickup truck, which she'd loaded with clippings and books and her own drawings. Stomping on the gas, she roared down the road in a puff of dirt and spitting gravel.

"Damn Dennis," she said, but then she stopped. "No, Dennis was a complete villain, but I don't regret this baby. She's mine, and we're going to have a good life together, no matter what I decide about Thomasina. I'll make her world special."

But words were cheap. Abby knew that better than anyone. What she wanted was a perfect world for her baby. So far she wasn't even close to being able to provide that. Money would help, and Griffin was going to pay her good money, but the fact was that she was going to have to work closely with the man to earn it. And she didn't want to. He made her itch. He made her self-conscious. Worse, he made her feel like a woman, and confound it, that was the last thing she wanted to feel.

So by the time she got to Griffin's house, Abby was in a fine frenzy. Don't make more of this than it is, she told herself. It's just a simple case of discontent with the lot life has given you this week, she argued. But then Griffin came into sight. He walked up to her truck, all smooth strides and lean muscles and killer smiles.

Darn! Not simple discontent, she admitted. Nothing about the prospect of working with Griffin was going to be easy. And what she was dealing with right now was a huge case of nerves.

He opened the door for her and held out his hand to help her out. She eyed his open palm, and for a horrid distressing moment pictured that palm sliding down her bare rib cage…and up again.

Okay, so she was having an attack of nerves *and* hormones, Abby thought, trying to hide her distress as she continued to hesitate. Blast. She was into her second trimester, and all the books said that sex became more intriguing then. That was the problem. She couldn't blame her new client, no matter how good he looked. No matter that when she took a deep breath, his compelling scent caught in her nostrils. Not his fault, she reminded herself. Hormones.

"Everything all right, Abby?" he asked.

She sucked in her lower lip and nodded. Poised on the edge of her seat, she turned and slid her hand into his, holding her breath as the sensation of touching him exploded inside her. Quickly she slipped from the truck and retrieved her hand.

"I'm just fine," she said, hoping that her voice came out clear and strong as she meant it to. "Are you ready to go over the property inch by inch?"

"I've set the morning aside. I'm all yours."

She blinked at that. He was talking about his time, of course. And as they tromped over the grounds surrounding the big, beautiful sea-green house, Abby began to relax.

"If I had the wherewithal to do anything I wanted, you'd have a pond right here," she pointed out.

He looked at the drawing she held. "That's about dead center of the pitching mound for the baseball field."

She gave him a sideways glance. ''I'm aware of that.''

He raised one brow. ''And you don't approve.''

''Not my business to approve or disapprove.''

Griffin let out a low laugh at that. ''Abby, I'm beginning to understand that you are one very opinionated woman. You may pretend not to pass judgment, but you clearly don't like the baseball field here. You have something against sports?''

In response, Abby bent down and picked up a rock. She pitched it at the nearest fence post and hit it dead center. With an agile movement, she picked up another rock and another, hurling them expertly and squarely at the fence post. They hit the wood with a satisfying thunk.

Griffin let out a low whistle.

Abby dusted off her hands. ''Pitcher, girls baseball, Red Rose High all four years that I attended. I like sports. I just like trees more.''

''I intend to have plenty of trees.''

''Most of them are at the edges of the property where they won't really count.'' She looked up at him earnestly, a low yearning she didn't want to examine—ever—filling her.

To her relief, he didn't smile or laugh or even frown.

''I want the landscaping to count,'' he said. ''That's why I hired you.''

''And I suppose maybe I'm being a little tough on you and your plans,'' she said, waving the drawings he'd given her. ''Maybe I'm just having trouble adjusting to the big changes you're planning. Change is unsettling.'' And change seemed to be the driving force in her life lately.

''Lots of things are unsettling,'' he argued. ''And

sometimes change can be positive. Other times it simply can't be helped.''

Oh, yeah. Lots of things *were* unsettling. This man, with his let-me-show-you-paradise eyes and sexy smile was. And, yes, change often couldn't be avoided. Strong as she was, she was powerless to stop the forces that had taken over her life.

''I need this to be right, Abby,'' Griffin said. ''Not just your vision, not just mine, but right for my purpose.''

Okay, she'd known that all along, she supposed. It was just that this house and these grounds represented an idyllic part of her childhood, and almost all of those rare and precious times had been swept away. She was still fighting the loss, and that just wasn't right. Wasn't she a professional, the best at what she did? Hadn't she promised Griff the best she had?

''Let's sit down and figure it out.'' And she took her pad of paper and plopped gracefully onto the grass.

Within minutes she and Griffin had their heads together and were arguing about the details.

''That's a lot more foliage than I'd anticipated,'' he said.

''Yes, but just look at what you get when we do this.'' Abby looked up at him, her hands moving in the way she couldn't seem to help when she explained herself, her maple-leaf earrings dangling and gently brushing her cheeks with her movements. ''If we set this up as a hub system with the fields radiating out and separated by gardened walkways, you'll get the best of both. There's plenty of land here.''

''But my main focus is supposed to be the business. When my clients walk out on the grounds, I want them to see a plethora of athletics going on.''

''They will. See?'' she said, pointing to the tennis courts, the swimming pools, the areas for football and track, baseball, soccer and basketball. ''When you're on the football field, you won't see the other sports because of the spokes of gardens and trees that separate the different areas, but from the back of the house, you can see it all. And it will look impressive, especially with the low maze at the hub of the wheel. This will be a stunning celebration of athletics and nature. That's what you wanted, wasn't it?''

Griffin rubbed the back of his neck. ''I suppose I didn't have your vision regarding the green space. I just didn't want it to look spartan, the way endless sports fields would. You're sure about all the gardens?''

She leaned back and crossed her arms. For a second she thought his gaze dropped to her breasts, but she must have been mistaken about that, because when she looked again, he was staring straight into her eyes. ''You said you wanted to bring clients here. Won't some of them bring their wives?''

Griffin twisted up his lips. ''That's a possibility.''

''And don't you think some of those wives might be more impressed by gorgeous grounds than an impressive horseshoe pit?''

He grinned. ''You think my clients would be influenced by their spouses' tastes? What about the female clients I have?''

''They don't like flowers?''

''Lots of them don't like to admit it. They feel it makes them look soft when they're competing in such a cutthroat, male-dominated field.''

''So the fact that you embrace both sides might make them feel that they don't have to choose one or the other, no? And don't lots of men appreciate ambiance, as well?''

Abby was leaning forward now. Griffin didn't answer.

''You don't think so?'' she asked hesitantly.

''I think whoever recommended you knew what they were talking about,'' he said, his voice low, his eyes intent.

Abby swallowed hard. ''I haven't even planted anything yet.''

''Don't be so sure of that,'' he said, and he got to his feet and helped her to hers. ''All right, I like your ideas.''

''Good. I think we should put a small koi pond over there,'' she said, gesturing to a small wooded area with a narrow trail leading into it. ''Good place for people to meditate on any important decisions they have to make. And of course the playground should be close to the house.''

''I don't sell playground equipment.''

''But you have a son, and some of this is for him, isn't it?''

The smile disappeared from his eyes. ''All of this is for him. If not for Casey, I wouldn't be here.''

''For the summers.''

''Yes.''

He bit the word out, and it was clear that there was bitterness involved in this summer arrangement with his son. She didn't ask what all this was about, but she desperately wanted to, and suddenly she, who was almost never at a loss for words, couldn't think of a thing to say.

''Let's go up to the house,'' he said suddenly, and his voice was rough and low. ''You need to eat.''

She glanced up at him, and she could swear that he was staring at her abdomen. Had someone told?

"I take care of myself," she said defensively.

"Good. Let's make that *I* need to eat, then."

And so there was nothing she could do except follow him up to the house. On the way there, he was silent. So was she, which meant that she had plenty of time to muse on the fact that most likely Griffin knew that she was pregnant. Unless he was completely obtuse and numb to everything going on around him, he had no doubt heard about the town's quest to bring men to the area. Of course he had. He was Parker's friend, and he had come to the open house the town had held. So, if he knew that the town was looking for men, and if he suspected that she was pregnant and single…

Abby stopped in her tracks. "We need to be clear on one thing, Griff. I believe in being perfectly blunt and honest. So you should know that this is just business for me. I'm not looking…that is, I don't want you to think that just because the town is doing this search… Well, the fact is that I am just not in the line for a romantic relationship, now or ever. You haven't said anything that indicated otherwise, but just in case it had crossed your mind that I might be thinking of you that way, I'm not."

Her face felt warm; she knew that her cheeks must be blooming red, which always looked just plain awful with her strawberry hair, but that couldn't be helped.

Another man might have laughed or teased or even sighed with relief. Griffin did none of those things. Instead he picked up a rock and threw it at the nearest fence post, where it struck with a resounding and satisfying thud.

"I wasn't thinking any of those things, although it

crossed my mind that you might be a woman alone at a time when most women don't want to be alone. How far along are you?''

''Four months.''

He took a deep breath. ''And you're okay with that?''

''I want the baby, yes. I don't want the father, which is just fine with him, because he doesn't want either of us.''

''So he was a bastard.''

''Pretty much, but then I can't blame him for everything. It takes two to make a baby.''

He stuck his hands in his pockets and nodded. ''For the record, I wasn't wondering if you were going to come on to me, because it was so clear that you weren't affected in the slightest. I don't want to sound immodest, but I have a fair amount of experience with women who want me. You didn't exhibit any of the signs. That's a good thing, because…well, I'm not a good bet in relationships. I'm fine starting out, but not so great in the long haul, no matter how much I want things to work. This last time—my marriage and then my divorce a year ago, the subsequent separation from my son when he's so young, barely four years old—it's just about killed me. I don't ever want to risk losing a child that way again. So Casey's it. No more wives, no more children, no more risks outside the corporate kind. That mostly ensures that Casey and I will be fine. I think you and I will be just fine, too.''

The smile he gave her was small and tight. She answered it with one of her own. ''We will,'' she said, knowing she should feel relief, and yet feeling a little regret just the same. He really was a beautiful, kind man. It was a shame no woman would ever get to share that. Or at least no woman would get to share it for the long term. She wasn't so innocent as to think that a man like Griffin would give up women entirely. When he looked at her, she could see that he was attracted and that he would like to touch.

No doubt he wouldn't touch her, because of their business relationship and because she was pregnant and had just told him in no uncertain terms that she didn't want him to.

But he would touch other women. An endless line of temporary women. As temporary as he would be to Red Rose.

He *was* here for just the summer.

"We'll be fine," she said suddenly, firmly. "When does your son arrive?"

Griffin's eyes lit up. "He'll be here in two days. I want his time here to be the best, Abby. His mother, Cheryl, insisted she needed him to go with her to her mother's, for a week at first, and then she insisted on another week. Otherwise I would have had him with me already. I could have fought her, but for such a little boy, he's seen too much fighting in his lifetime. Still, I won't let it happen again. I don't ever want him to think I don't want him with me every minute."

She could hear the regret in his voice, and the bitterness.

Abby couldn't help herself then. She touched Griffin's sleeve. "He's going to love this place. It's special." Her voice was a whisper. She looked up and realized that she had moved closer than she'd meant to.

Griffin reached out. With the tip of one finger, he tucked back a loose strand of her hair, smoothing it behind her neck, his touch sending a shiver through her. His eyes drifted to her eyes, to her lips. He looked down to where her hand still rested against his arm, and she felt suddenly self-conscious and forward. Abby snatched her hand back, but he caught it.

As her skin turned warm, he turned her hand over and stared at the palm. Gently he stroked his thumb over it.

"He is going to love this place. We're going to make it special, you and I, Abby. That's one pact we can make together."

And then he folded his hand around hers, his grip warm and strong as he led her to his house. She couldn't tell if the churning of her stomach was her baby making her presence known or if it was her own reaction to the man. Either guess was a good bet, and one of those reasons was just plain reckless.

Maybe if she finalized her deal with Thomasina, dealing with Griffin would be easier.

Chapter Three

The next morning Abby pulled up in front of Thomasina Edgerton's house and reluctantly started up the front walk. In basic style, Thomasina's house looked like a lot of others in Red Rose, a small-frame Cape Cod with carefully tended roses blooming out front. But Thomasina's white mailbox was decorated with scattered pink hearts, and on her lawn was a wrought-iron ornament of a man and woman each bending forward from the waist so that their lips just touched. She also had a small sign outside her door that said Romance Consultant. Abby frowned at the sign. She'd seen it hundreds of times before, but before it had never held any significance for her. This time it did.

Abby reluctantly raised her hand to knock on the door, but it opened before she had the chance. Thomasina stood there, her brown hair in a knot on top of her head, soft tendrils slipping out around her narrow face. Her eyes sparkled and there was a look of anticipation on her face.

"I'm glad you've finally decided to come. This is going to be so much fun, Abby."

Fun? Not a chance. Abby suddenly wished she could find some blight on Thomasina's roses so she could say that she was only stopping by as a professional courtesy. Unfortunately, Thomasina had a gift for growing roses. Not a single spot marred hers. There was no excuse for backing down now.

"I don't want fun, Tommy. I need a father for my baby."

Thomasina glowed. "And that's just what we're going to find you. Come into the kitchen. I've made a pot of tea." She turned and led the way. Abby noted once again that Thomasina's house was a lot like her: sparkling and a bit old-fashioned in appearance. It would be easy to imagine Tommy Edgerton living in Victorian times, but then, maybe it was just the whole matchmaker business and her endless optimism that made her seem more innocent and out of date.

"I can't stay long, Tommy. I've got tons of work to do."

"I've heard. You're working for Mr. O'Dell. What a hunk."

The word hunk didn't seem to fit Tommy's vocabulary. If she had said dream boat, that would have fit, but in any case, either term would have been accurate where Griff was concerned.

"Don't you think so?" Tommy asked. She grinned at Abby.

"He's very nice looking," Abby said primly, when she was never prim.

Tommy chuckled. "He's fascinating. They say he has the Midas touch when it comes to business. He's started up and sold several companies, and always at a huge profit. And women...well they just fall all over him." She sighed, and then she seemed to shake off her romantic notions as she sat up straighter. "Oh, well, I wish I could get him to list with me, but I'm afraid he's off-limits."

Abby's heartbeat picked up to panic tempo. "You didn't talk to him about matching him up with me, did you?"

A frown creased Tommy's forehead. "I don't discuss my clients with strangers, Abby. Or even with locals who aren't clients." At Abby's confused look, she shook her head. "Mr. O'Dell is not a client nor is he apparently ever going to be. He explained to me that he isn't remotely interested in acquiring a wife or in any romantic dealings."

Which Abby already knew, but the mere fact that Tommy had approached him...

"I only discuss you with the men I try to match you with, Abby," Tommy said firmly. "That's my rule. And I'm only discussing Mr. O'Dell because so many women have asked about him. I wanted to be up-front about what you could expect. We're definitely going to find you someone, but we may have to look outside the town of Red Rose. I wanted you to know that."

Good. Tommy's voice and expression had turned businesslike. The dreamy romantic had been shelved for now. Abby sat down and prepared for the ordeal. Tommy picked up a clipboard. "Now I need to know just what you're looking for, what your expectations are and what you feel are your own assets. We want this match to be perfect, to be all that you and your partner are dreaming of."

Abby took a deep breath and shook her head. "First of all, Tommy, I have to be very honest with you.

You've always been honest with me, and you should know that this search has nothing to do with dreams. I don't want love or romance, hearts and flowers or courtship, and I can't offer those things, either."

For a second Tommy's brown eyes looked stricken. "Surely you want something from the man?"

"I want a partner and a father for my baby. That's all."

"Sounds kind of dry."

"I'm kind of dry, Tommy."

Her friend looked skeptical. She studied Abby carefully and touched a strand of her red hair, which she'd often been told reflected her personality perfectly. "I would have called you fiery."

"You would have the entire world paired up and in love, Tommy," Abby said gently. "Which is fine for most, but not for me. I just—well, I just can't go that route again."

She looked up from her speech to see sympathy darkening Tommy's eyes. Oh, that just wouldn't do at all. "Let's face it, Tommy, I'm pushy, I'm stubborn, I'm not an easy woman to get along with. I need a man to be a friend and a father, someone who wants a simple family life without all the romantic frills."

"All right, but that makes it much tougher. Most men want a lot more."

When she said the words *a lot more,* Tommy's tone indicated that she was discussing sex. Somehow the reference just didn't fit her personality, and Abby half expected a deep blush that never came. As sure as her name began with an *A,* Abby couldn't think of anyone who was much more innocent than Thomasina. The thought that she would have even an inkling of what most men wanted almost made Abby want to laugh. But then, why was she here if she didn't think Tommy could help?

"Because I'm desperate," she muttered to herself.

"What? I didn't catch that." Her friend leaned forward.

"It wasn't important. I'll try to be as cooperative as I can," Abby said. And she did try. She and Tommy made a list of what she considered her good points and bad points. And then Tommy opened her "book of opportunities." Inside was a page and a photo of each man who had come to her. Truth to tell there weren't many. Truth to tell, Abby felt slightly nauseous when Tommy took her picture with the obvious intent of making her own page in a similar book.

"Well, we have Dwight Zaynor, but he's kind of quiet," Tommy said with a frown. "You might eat him alive."

And if sweet, innocent Tommy thought the man was too meek for her, he no doubt was. Abby turned the page.

"Jeff Seeton," Tommy said. "Former high school football player. He came here looking for a wife, he said, but I think he's just looking for sex. He keeps trying to peer down my blouse." Which was pretty funny considering the fact that Tommy favored high-neck blouses trimmed in lace. Nevertheless, she obviously didn't think highly of Jeff Seeton, and she pursed her lips and firmly turned the page.

In less than ten minutes time, Tommy had gone through the thin book. "But don't be discouraged," she insisted. "Now that you've signed up for real, I'll be on the lookout for the right man. He doesn't have to come to me."

Which meant what? That Tommy would be accosting

men on the street asking them if they'd like to hook up with Abigail Chesney? For once in her life, Abby didn't have the guts to ask, especially when she was pretty sure she knew the answer.

"Maybe we should just forget this," she muttered.

Tommy got a cool look in her eyes. "I never knew you to be fainthearted, Abby, and I know you want this for your baby. Do not get squeamish on me now. I know what I'm doing."

And to say anything more would have been to hurt the feelings of a tenderhearted woman and a friend.

Abby did her best to smile and to thank Tommy as she made her way out to her truck. It was only when she was safely away and on the open road that she allowed herself to let loose and yell. She even tried out a few curse words she ordinarily would never have uttered.

When she was done, she realized that her truck was pointed in the direction of Griffin's house.

As if things weren't bad enough, now she appeared to have a homing beacon where her boss was concerned. Guided by what could only be misplaced lust, she was drawn to the man.

Turn the truck around and go home, she ordered herself.

"No, I want to get this job over with and done," she said aloud to herself. "Because once it's done I can stop even thinking about him. And maybe then I can really concentrate on helping Tommy out." It was the first time since she'd stepped into the house that she admitted she'd been judging every man that Tommy had shown her against the man she was headed toward right now.

"You are an idiot, Abby," she said. "You don't even

know the man, and what you know only proves that you two would have to both be brain dead and reckless to get involved on any level.'' And, as always, there was no one around to contradict her. All too soon Griffin's house came into sight.

But I will not go near the house, she thought. I'll go out to the fields and start planting those poplars I had sent over. That should get my thoughts and my day back on the right track. For sure, she was not going to venture near Griffin. She couldn't believe that Tommy had tried to set him up with a wife.

Griffin wanted to put his fist through several hard walls. Cheryl had just called to say she would be one more day late getting Casey to him, because she'd told him he could have a friend sleep over tomorrow night. As if she hadn't already been two weeks late in delivering his son to him. And she'd said it with that tone of voice that showed she knew he wouldn't fight her when doing so would deprive his child of a treat.

What he needed was a distraction, a task to focus his energies on. And when he looked out his window and saw Abby's baby-blue truck, he figured he might as well join her. Maybe he could be of some use.

That excuse sure sounded good, anyway.

So he marched across the lawn toward her. When he got close enough, he could see that she was wielding a shovel. Or maybe attacking the earth would be a better description of what she was doing.

''What on earth was I thinking? Am I totally out of my mind?'' she asked herself, stabbing the shovel into the soft dirt.

''It's not that. I'm just…darn it,'' she said, answering herself, and she raised the shovel again, with less care this time. If she didn't slow down, she was going to hurt herself. Griff didn't want to intrude on her private conversation or her thoughts, but he just couldn't see standing by while she let her mood run wild and did some serious damage to her foot or some other precious body part. And lately he knew too much about blinding anger not to recognize it in someone else.

"You're just what?" he asked, taking several long strides to bring himself up beside her.

"I'm—what?" Abby froze in midstab. She looked up at him, her eyes unfocused, her red hair a wild soft tangle of curls. "Griff, I'm sorry. I didn't know you were here."

"That was pretty obvious. Want me to beat someone up for you?"

"Who?"

"Whoever you've been pretending this plot of ground is."

Slowly her eyes zeroed in on him. She shook her head slowly. "It's me I'm mad at."

"Mind if I ask why?"

She shrugged. "A potentially bad decision I've made."

"Hiring on with me?"

For a moment she hesitated. He thought she was going to say yes. He also thought she looked very pretty in her dazed and confused and slightly embarrassed state.

"Not really," she finally said. "You knew I was reluctant to take on this job, but that's not what's got me upset."

"And it's none of my business, anyway. Is that it?"

A trace of a smile flitted across her lips and then disappeared. "It's none of your business, but this is Red

Rose. You'll hear about it sooner or later. I'd rather you heard about it from me, because if you don't, you're going to think that your new landscaper is crazy. You'll wonder why you hired someone who would do something so irrational."

"Sounds bad. So you maimed someone? Or stole a pickup truck? Or ran down the streets of town wearing nothing but a sprig of ivy?

For a second she colored up. Then she actually smiled at him. "If you're trying to make me feel better, it's almost working, but no, I'm afraid it's worse than that. I've hired the local matchmaker to find me a husband."

Okay, so hitting him on the head with the shovel would have stunned him less. Griffin blinked.

"You?"

She visibly bristled. "You think no one will want to marry me?"

"Whoa, you know that's not it."

She dropped her shovel and planted her hands on her hips. "I don't know. I don't really know what you think, since I don't really know you."

"All right, then. I think that there are probably many men who would love to get the chance to cohabitate with you, to marry you, to share a cottage with you. I just thought you weren't into that kind of thing. You said so, more or less."

"I said I didn't want romance or serious relationships, and I don't, but I'm going to have a baby, as we've discussed. I want that baby to have two parents. And so I've asked Thomasina, the local matchmaker, to find someone for us. Is there anything wrong with that?"

She raised her chin. Although she had been haranguing herself just moments earlier, it was clear that now she was daring him to criticize her choices.

Was there anything wrong with her decision? Only about a hundred things he could think of. In the short time since he'd met her, he'd already decided that she was a woman of beauty and fire. She was a woman a man would dream of in his bed. If she thought some nameless, faceless man was going to be satisfied with holding hands or with less, then she was just too innocent for words. But maybe he'd misunderstood.

"Are you intending for it to be a real marriage?" He raked her with his eyes, leaving no doubt what he was talking about.

"That's none of your business."

"You just made it my business. You told me I'd know all your secrets in a small town."

"Not those behind-closed-doors kind of secrets." But her voice lacked its customary conviction.

"Abby," he said softly. "Have you really thought this through completely? Could you take a man into your bed just to get a father for your baby?"

She bit her lip, but she didn't back down or look away. "I don't exactly know. I guess I'll decide when I meet the man."

He took a step closer, the anger of these past few weeks rising to the surface. "Abby, this is a big step. There's so much at stake here. Being married to the wrong person can create all kinds of hell and not just for you and the man. I know what I'm talking about. Think carefully."

"I will." She swallowed.

He took another step near her. "I mean it. Think ahead to what marriage with the wrong person could really mean."

She nodded again. ''I'm trying.'' Her breath came a little faster.

He took one last step and now he was completely in her space, his thighs almost up against hers. ''Marriage is the most intimate of relationships,'' he said, his voice low. ''Think about what it would be like to have a total stranger, someone like me, for instance, demand to touch you in a way you might not like.''

And he slowly lowered his head. He hovered there, waiting for her to tell him to back off. When she didn't, he cupped her jaw with one hand, holding her still as his mouth covered hers, as he finally touched her.

She was soft and delicious and warm. When their lips met, she sighed just a little, the tiniest of sounds. She swayed toward him slightly. He was barely touching her. It was the lightest of kisses, and yet he felt his control start to slide and tilt. He wanted to pull her into his arms and start the fire. For a second he thought he felt her hands on his chest. Pulling him closer? Maybe. Maybe not.

His mind was going fuzzy, but…not completely. Somewhere, somehow, he knew this was Abby. He knew she'd told him she didn't want this kind of thing. He knew he'd had a purpose here, but what the hell had it been? Whatever it was, this was wrong.

The thought brought him straight back to reality, and he released her immediately.

She stood there, hair disheveled, lips rosy and moist, blue eyes haunted.

''Abby, I'm sorry. Heck, what in hell was I thinking? He shoved his hand back through his hair.

''I believe you were trying to make a point,'' she said, her voice trembling as she held out one shaky hand.

He swore beneath his breath. "I—damn, I thought so at first, but any way you look at it, it was a bad idea."

"It was." He thought he saw her look at his lips, maybe even shiver.

Had he scared her? It was hard to tell with a woman like Abby, who was so set on letting the world know that nothing fazed her. "I promise you, I'm not prone to pouncing on women," he said. "You won't have to worry about me again."

She raised her chin. "You didn't pounce. You weren't exactly holding me in a head lock. You were barely even touching me. I could have easily moved away."

"You sure? As you said, you don't really know me."

"No, but a man who is concerned enough about the possibility that I might ruin my life doing something stupid wouldn't be likely to kiss me against my will."

"Maybe not, but the fact is that I shouldn't have kissed you at all."

"I believe you were just showing me that if I entered into a loveless marriage arranged by Thomasina, then I needed to be prepared for intimacy with a man I barely knew."

Yes, that was exactly what he'd told himself. But that wasn't the total truth.

He shook his head. "I might have implied that, I might even have had such an arrogant thought. Maybe I even thought that was what I was doing for half a minute, but in the end, that was a lie. The truth is that I wouldn't be so condescending as to try to teach you a lesson. You're too independent a lady for that."

She smiled then. "Thank you for realizing that I have to make my own decisions."

"Okay, but..."

She cocked her head. "But what?"

"Promise me you'll be careful? And that if you ever run up against a guy who proves to be too much physically for you to handle that you'll let me break his nose?"

She chuckled. "I promise, but I assure you that I can handle things myself. I always have. I've always had to, all my life. I don't see why things should change now."

That should have reassured Griffin, he thought later that day, but somehow it didn't.

Still, he had promised to let her make her own decisions. And stranger that he was, he didn't have any right to interfere in her life, especially not her love life.

So what was he going to do?

Leave her alone, he told himself. She hadn't pursued his reasons for kissing her, and that was good, since he didn't want to pursue them himself. All he knew was that touching her again would only lead them both down the road to heartache and madness and tons of trouble, so he would do his darnedest to keep his distance.

But, heavens, the woman was alone and pregnant and seeing a matchmaker who was going to set her up with who knew what kind of men? Parker had already told him that there weren't many good men left in town. What did that say for the kind of men Abby's matchmaker would be sending her way?

Griffin didn't know. Maybe he needed to have another talk with Thomasina Edgerton. Not to interfere, of course. Abby was really none of his business, she'd certainly send sparks flying his way if he thought she was overstepping the line, but, heck, it wasn't that at all. It was…well, a man should just know things about the town he'd just bought into.

Shouldn't he?

There certainly couldn't be any harm in just asking a few questions.

Chapter Four

Griffin had a bad feeling the minute Thomasina opened her door the next day. "I'm not looking for a wife," he said, and then immediately felt foolish when the woman grinned.

"So you told me earlier. That implies you're looking for something else, Mr. O'Dell. What exactly is it?"

There was something knowing about the look she gave him that made him feel like an awkward young man who should be shifting in his shoes on her doorstep. And that just wasn't his way and never had been. Griffin leveled a stare at her. "I'm here for information, Ms. Edgerton. I have reason to believe you can supply it."

"I don't discuss my clients, Mr. O'Dell."

"One of your clients works for me."

"I'm aware of that. It doesn't matter."

"It does to me. You may be putting her in danger. She's in a delicate position. I wouldn't like to see any harm come to her."

''I would never willingly put her in harm's way.'' The lady's mouth was a thin line. She crossed her arms and leveled a stare at him.

''Maybe you wouldn't know you were doing that. Men can be real jerks at times.''

She raised a brow.

''I'm not excluding myself,'' he agreed.

Thomasina unbent. ''Why do you care what happens to Abby? You don't know her. You've only just moved to town, and you're not going to be here permanently.'' She waited, a speculative look in her eyes.

''Don't even think it,'' he told her. ''It's not like that and never will be. But Abby's a woman alone, and soon she'll have a baby. That can be a scary place for a woman to be. I won't lie and say that I approve of the matchmaking business. I don't, but obviously Abby has already made the choice to sign with you. All I'm trying to do is make sure nothing bad happens to her.

''These are tough times for her. Push her together with the wrong type of man, and she might make a hasty and ill-advised decision.'' Like his wife had. ''She might be willing to settle for a man who would be disastrously ill-suited for her. That could be tragic. And…'' He hesitated, looking at the woman's prim high collar and hopelessly romantic house. ''I don't mean to be blunt, Ms. Edgerton, but I'm not sure you've considered the fact that some men might take advantage of Abby's situation.''

''I wouldn't let that happen.''

''You might not be able to stop it, and frankly Ms. Edgerton—'' he looked at the wrought iron boy and girl on her lawn ''—you might not see it coming the way a man might.''

Her eyes widened slightly. "Are you asking me to let you know who I'm setting Abby up with?"

He remembered how Abby had felt against him. He thought of some other man pressing her that way and not stopping when she wanted him to. "That would be a very good idea."

"No, it wouldn't. Furthermore, it's not going to happen, Mr. O'Dell. Even if I approved of your methods, which I don't, I'd never do it. It would be a breach of professionalism. It's insulting to Abby."

Griffin blinked, and reality set in. She was right. He had no business micromanaging Abby's love life.

"I don't want to insult Abby," he agreed. "But I would like to ensure her safety. Can you promise she'll be safe with the men you set her up with?"

Thomasina hesitated. "I do my best to ask a lot of questions and get to know my clients' minds, to know as much about each of them as I can before I set them up together."

"You didn't answer my question, Ms. Edgerton."

"I answered it the best that I could, Mr. O'Dell. I'm not going to feed you information about Abby's prospective dates. I'm not giving you boycott power. That is what you're asking for, isn't it?"

Okay, so maybe the woman had a house covered in hearts. She obviously wasn't letting herself be blinded by stars in her eyes. Once again Griffin amazed himself with his inability to read a woman's mind. Not that he cared to read just any woman's mind.

A picture of Abby attacking the ground and talking to herself presented itself to him. The touch of her lips, hot against his, made him shift and fight to ignore the sensation.

The matchmaker was right. He was letting the situation run away with him. He really had no business asking anything about Abby, other than those things that had to do with her work.

He nodded to Thomasina. ''My apologies for overstepping the boundaries, Ms. Edgerton,'' he said. ''I respect your work ethic, but if you can't bring yourself to confide in me, you might mention to any of those men you send her way that I would take a personal interest in confronting any man who didn't treat her with respect.''

She studied him for a second, a frown on her forehead. Finally she nodded slightly. ''*That* I might be able to do.''

Griffin breathed easier. ''Thank you.'' He turned to go down the stairs and retrace his steps to his car.

''I will be very careful with her,'' Thomasina called after him. ''That's a promise. Abby will be a difficult match to make, but I would never cut corners or try to force someone inappropriate on her.''

Griffin stopped. He looked back over his shoulder. ''Why difficult?''

Thomasina shrugged. ''It won't be a conventional marriage, and to say more than that, Mr. O'Dell, would be a disturbing breach of confidence, so don't ask any more questions. By the way…''

He waited.

''If you do change your mind, I'll begin a search for you, Mr. O'Dell. There are plenty of women in town who'd like to start something with you. I've already had requests.''

He laughed and shook his head. ''Afraid I'm not a good choice, Ms. Edgerton. I'm the very kind of man I'm asking you to warn away from Abby. There won't be any wives for me.'' This wasn't the kind of town where a man started something with a woman when he didn't intend to finish it, and finish it right.

And once again Griffin tasted the sweetness of Abby's lips. He wondered how many of Thomasina's men would taste Abby before this was through.

The thought nearly spun him around with the intention of warning Thomasina one more time.

But when he looked up, she'd closed her door. Maybe she was right. Abby wanted a husband, and most people seemed to think she needed one. Who was he to make that search more difficult for her?

Nobody. In fact, Ms. Thomasina Edgerton was right. He shouldn't be interfering at all. Abby was nothing to him but an employee, and it was pure folly to think of her as anything else.

Well, Abby thought the next day, things were certainly going well. She was just starting on the gardens, but she had made all of her plans, ordered all her supplies and was setting up her crew's work schedule for the days to come when the heavy work would set in. More important, though, she seemed to have gotten past that kiss. Hardly even caught herself touching her lips anymore. Or thinking about it. Not like two days ago.

And just like that, she was plastered up against Griffin's chest again, his warmth against hers, his mouth driving her wild.

Her lips tingled, her face flamed, her body reacted and she remembered how she'd almost lost herself and made the mistake of pressing herself closer into Griffin's arms. The man had merely been trying to warn her away from getting involved with strange men. How humiliating, and how awful that she'd wanted him so badly. If he were here right now…

She looked up hastily. All she heard was the sound of wind in the nearby oak trees. All she saw was the long expanse of green fields and the house standing tall and silent. No sign of Griffin, just as there hadn't been all day today or most of the day before. He had only come out long enough to tell her that his son's arrival would be delayed by a day and that he had to meet with some contractors.

"Good," she said aloud, staking out a flower bed. "Solitude is what I want, after all, isn't it? Just lots of work and lots of time and space to do it in, and no distractions. The man kept his word."

Sunny had told her that she'd seen Griffin standing on Thomasina Edgerton's doorstep, but when she'd mentioned his name to Thomasina, the woman had frowned at her.

"I told you I don't discuss my clients, Abby."

Abby's breath had caught. "Griffin's a client now?"

Thomasina had shook her head. "No. That is, he says no, but maybe someday…right now he's adamant that he doesn't want to marry."

And every woman in Red Rose was hoping that someday would come soon. Did Thomasina feel that way, too?

A small spark of shame at the town she loved and the ladies she loved slipped in. "Don't pressure him, all right, Tommy?"

Thomasina laughed. "I don't think he's a man to be pressured into marriage."

Which implied that some men were.

"Don't pressure anyone to marry me, either, okay? It has to be voluntarily. Otherwise…" She didn't finish. She didn't have to. The fact that she didn't want a repeat performance of her father came through.

"I won't pressure anyone, Abby," Thomasina said.

But if that was true, then why had Griffin been standing on Thomasina's doorstep?

"Maybe he just likes her, idiot," Abby said. "He's a man, after all." And he was a man who liked to kiss.

Abby stabbed at a weed, a bit harder than necessary.

"Whoever he is, I wouldn't want to be him." Griffin's voice sounded deep behind her, and Abby sprang up and whirled to face him, scrubbing dirt from her pants.

"Careful," he said, catching her as she swayed slightly. "A pregnant woman gets dizzy sometimes."

"I don't. Nothing bothers me." Which was a bald-faced lie, but one she just had to say. "Why are you here? Is there something you wanted to add to the plans? Something you need?"

His eyes grew dark, but he shook his head. "No, just someone I wanted you to meet. You can come out now, Case. This is Abby, and I promise you, she's not going to stab you with her weeder."

He looked back, and immediately Abby turned toward the nearest oak tree. A small hand was visible, a few tufts of thick dark hair, and two large gray eyes peeking out. Worried eyes.

Abby dropped the pronged tool she still held.

"I'm only dangerous if you're a dandelion," she said, smiling at the little boy. "Or an outlaw."

A mouth appeared, smiling a tiny bit. The little boy edged carefully away from the tree. "Not an outlaw. Not a bad guy, neither."

"Me, neither," she said.

"Dad tode me you do...you're a lan...lan—"

"Landscaper," she supplied. "That's a fancy name for someone who makes designs with plants."

"Whatcha makin' now?" he asked, looking where she had been working.

What she was making was a garden of blue larkspur and borage, interspersed with golden calendulas and nasturtium, surrounded by a border of snowy ageratum. That didn't sound like something a four-year-old would care to discuss.

"I'm making a hole first of all," she said. "Want to help?"

The little boy's eyes lit up. "I like holes. Big ones. This gonna be a big one?"

Abby looked at her trays of flowers, none that required a very large hole.

"An enormous one. A whopper," she agreed. She could always fill in and redo later, but how often did one have a chance to delight and comfort a nervous four-year-old who had seen too many tough times in his short little life?

Griffin chuckled, and when she glanced up to look at him, he mouthed the words "Thank you." His eyes were like dark silver stars, burning into her.

She struggled to swallow. "Would you—would you like to help?" she offered. "After all, this is Casey's initiation to his new home. We should plant something in his honor." And suddenly she realized that she would plant something larger here. "Planting something makes a place special," she explained. "Taking care of it later makes the place even more special. It makes it yours. This will be yours and Casey's. If you like."

In answer, Griffin dropped to his knees beside her. He was wearing stone-colored pants, and the grass was slightly damp.

"Oh, they'll stain," she said, reaching for a knee pad. "I should have thought, but I—" She glanced down at her own old, ripped and faded jeans, her usual garb. Usually there was no need to take care. ''Let me just—'' She hastily placed the pad on the ground.

Griffin touched her arm, the skin bare beneath the sleeve of her T-shirt. ''Don't worry, Abby. They're just pants. It's just grass. Case and I don't get enough opportunities to roll around in the stuff. We'll be fine. It'll be good to get dirty together. Right, Tiger?''

His son smiled up at him. ''Me and Dad like dirt,'' he agreed.

Abby smiled, too, but she was intensely aware of Griffin's fingertips on her skin, his hand large and warm, her nerve endings far too responsive. She was horribly afraid that her breath was coming fast and that her chest was doing that telltale rising and falling thing that always let a man know that a woman was reacting to his touch.

She cleared her throat and scooted back a few inches, breaking the contact. ''Well then, let's get you some shovels,'' she said, rising to her feet and rushing to her truck.

For several seconds she rummaged through her tools, but when she whirled around holding a small spade for Casey and a larger shovel for Griffin, she stared right into Griff's eyes. He raised one brow and looked at her arm where he had been touching her only seconds ago. She felt the blush warm her. All right, so she was horribly transparent.

''I promised you'd be safe,'' he said. ''I meant that.''

And she knew what he meant. He thought she was afraid that he would kiss her again.

''I wasn't worried,'' she replied. And she hadn't been. Not that he would attack her, only that he would see that she couldn't seem to control her own reaction to him. Hell's bells, it was long past time she got back into the dating scene. She should have contacted Thomasina as soon as Dennis had left town. At least that way, being touched by a man would be no big deal anymore.

Griffin looked unconvinced.

Abby took a deep breath, placed a stubborn frown on her face and handed the shovel to Griffin. Deliberately she let her fingers feather over his. Lightly, a friendly touch, she told herself. A meaningless touch, the kind of things people came across all the time when they were passing objects from one person to the other.

Those kinds of touches didn't mean anything, any more than Griffin's earlier one had meant. She had to let him know that she wasn't susceptible to such things. He wasn't going to have to worry that she was going to be like the rest of the women in town, getting romantic ideas about him and giggling and simpering every time he said hello.

Don't feel, don't react to the warmth of his skin. Above all, don't blush, she ordered herself as she drew her hand away. And she stared deliberately, stubbornly straight into his eyes. ''I wasn't concerned,'' she said. ''That wasn't why I jumped up. We just needed these shovels.'' And then, because she absolutely couldn't keep staring into those arresting silver eyes anymore without losing her composure, she turned to the little boy who was waiting patiently for his shovel.

''Ready to get hot and sweaty and make a huge mess, Casey?'' she asked, relieved to be able to give the little boy a genuine smile.

Casey looked up at her with eager eyes. ''What can we put in the hole?''

Abby thought carefully. She almost said a burning

bush, because the plant's bright leaves would be impressive even to a child, but then she realized that Casey and Griffin would be gone by the time fall came around and the bush took on its crimson hues. Whatever they planted had to put on its show in summer.

"A butterfly bush, I think," she said, using its common term.

"It grows butterflies?" Casey asked.

Abby's eyes met Griffin's delighted ones. "It attracts butterflies," she explained, dropping to her knees beside Casey. "Will you like that?"

She hoped he wasn't afraid of the pretty insects. Some young children were.

"I like that," Casey said, his little body wriggling as he ran to Griffin. "Dad, let's dig. Gonna have butterflies."

"That's a great idea," Griffin agreed. But as his gaze met hers in a warm look of appreciation just before he turned to his son and began to help him clear the earth away, Abby knew that she wouldn't have to wait long for the butterflies to appear.

They were already here.

Chapter Five

A short time later Griffin looked over to see that his son had lain down on the grass and fallen asleep, his little head cradled in his arms.

"Almost done," Abby said, and she turned to look at him. He nodded toward Casey.

"Oh my, when did that happen?" she asked, and her eyes grew wide and worried.

"Probably when we were struggling to remove that big root that was blocking our way."

"And I didn't even notice?"

"You were busy. I didn't notice, either, and I'm his father, Abby. I'm not—it's been a long time. Too long. I forget his schedules, his routines. He's a busy guy, and he still needs a nap now and then." Griffin glanced at his watch. "Probably about a half hour ago."

"I'm so sorry," Abby began. She slid her hands down her long legs, wiping them on her jeans. "We can't just leave him there. He must be so uncomfortable."

Griffin shook his head. "I don't think so. Did you ever see a bigger smile on a sleeping child?"

Abby didn't answer, and Griffin wondered what that meant. That she hadn't had much experience with children? That she was worried about her impending motherhood? Cheryl had been. She'd fretted constantly throughout her pregnancy. Griffin was ashamed to think of the hours he'd been working during that time. He definitely hadn't been there for her. He hadn't been all that responsive to her needs. "Come on," he said, picking Casey up in his arms and starting toward the house.

"Oh no, I should finish here. Someone might trip."

Griffin stopped. "No one here but you and me and Casey, and he's asleep. Come eat."

"I'm dirty."

"Me, too."

"Casey needs quiet."

"It's a big house. He'll get quiet."

She hesitated, and Griffin felt a sharp shaft of anger rise up. At himself. She was nervous with him. She'd been nervous ever since he'd placed his lips on hers, and for that he could have kicked himself in the pants.

"Abby, I promised I wouldn't—"

He didn't even get to finish before she had hurried up to his side and began walking toward the house. "I told you I wasn't worried about that."

Yes, she was very adamant that she hadn't been affected at all by him. Maybe he should listen to her. She might not like hanging around with men who jumped her, but she sure didn't want him to think that she'd been in any way discomposed by his touch. Which probably meant that she was trying to be kind and maintain a business relationship with him, and he was making it tough for her.

''Just lunch. Then you can get back to your buddies,'' he told her.

''My buddies?''

He smiled and rested his hand on Casey's slim little spine. ''Yes, you were talking to that plot of ground the other day, or maybe it was the wind or the clouds you were conversing with. I assume you talk to your plants, too.''

Abby frowned. Then she shrugged sheepishly. ''It's good for them.''

''What do you tell them?''

She looked at him, a question in her eyes.

''I'm not teasing,'' he said. ''I'm serious. What do you tell a plant that helps it along?''

''Sometimes I just encourage them to grow or to turn their faces to the sun. Sometimes I promise to take care of them. Sometimes I just talk to them about whatever is on my mind. Now and then I sing to them. Or maybe I'm just talking and singing to myself, but it sure can't hurt either one of us. At least, I don't think so. There really is some evidence that suggests that plants respond to soothing noises.''

''Everyone says you're a genius with growing things. Whatever you're doing appears to work.''

He shifted Casey in his arms and cuddled him closer.

''You miss him a great deal, don't you?'' she asked softly.

''It's like death every time I have to let him go,'' he whispered, just in case his son should wake up and hear. He always made an effort to appear cheerful when they said their goodbyes. ''I don't remember ever having this kind of pain before until now. I don't ever want to experience it again.''

Abby nodded. ''Thomasina told me she was trying

to talk you into signing on with her. For the record, I asked her not to pressure you. This is going to be your summer home, and Casey's, too. It should be like home when you go into town. You shouldn't have to feel as if you're dodging most of the population of Red Rose. Everyone should have the right to choose whether they want to be paired up or not."

Her eyes were very blue and earnest. He supposed she'd had her share of people urging her to pair up with a man since everyone knew about her pregnancy.

He nodded. "I appreciate the thought. I'm not afraid of Thomasina, though, or any of my neighbors."

"Good, I'm glad. Tommy's my friend, and I love her to death. Sometimes, though, she gets so tied up in wanting to make the future right, that she doesn't think about the past and how it affects people."

"Yes, well, we'd be fools to ignore the past," he said gently. "It often tells us things about ourselves. Things we need to know and understand and learn from."

Abby glanced down to where he was gently brushing his fingers against his son's hair.

"You're good with him," she said softly. "I saw how you watched him when we were working, and how he looked to you, measuring your every response. He clearly adores you."

"Thank heavens," Griffin said, as they climbed the broad white steps to the house. "He's all I'll ever have."

Abby took a deep breath as she entered the Red Rose Café two days later. She hadn't been back in here since the day that Griffin had come to town to hire her. He was obviously still the main topic of interest, especially now that his workers and contractors were swarming the town. People were going to want to ask her questions. And she definitely didn't want to talk about Griffin. Heavens, she didn't even want to think about him. Doing so only made her feel all weak and feminine and totally stupid for feeling that way. She was getting to be as bad as those Victorian ladies that Tommy was so enamored of, the ones who swooned if a man so much as looked in their direction.

''It's good to see you, hon,'' Lydia said, plopping a cup of decaf in front of Abby. ''You've probably been working too hard.''

''Or thinking too hard,'' a soft voice said, and Abby looked up to see Ellie Donahue studying her with worried gray eyes. ''Is everything going smoothly with Griffin?''

''He's a man, isn't he?'' Sunny asked. ''Things never go well with men. At least not at first.'' But Abby noticed that Chester Atchison was hovering near Sunny, and that he gave Sunny a warm, knowing smile, tipping his ten-gallon hat back on his head.

''If things went too well, it wouldn't be any fun, would it, love?'' he asked.

Sunny, who had probably never blushed in her life, turned a deep pink. And she didn't object when Chester placed his big hand at her waist.

Abby's eyes slid to Chester's hand.

''I think she's finally beginning to believe that I like her bossy ways. In fact, I like everything about her. She's a lot of woman, and all of it is good,'' he explained. ''I sure don't need any other women to keep me satisfied. So maybe not all men are scum,'' he said with a smile. ''Right, Parker?''

Abby looked up to see Parker Monroe, tall, handsome and amber-eyed, exiting the part of the diner where

Lydia had fixed up an extra dining room to accommodate the anticipated influx of men to the town.

''I'm not sure what we're talking about. Did I hear you mention Griffin's name, sweetheart?'' he asked, smiling at Ellie and coming up to loop his arms around her and rest his chin on the top of her brown hair. ''I haven't been out there in a few days. Knowing Griffin, things are going full tilt. The man is a complete genius where business is concerned. Creating a demonstration model for his clients is a great plan, and I have no doubt that it will be a hit with the lucky clients he invites there, but it is a bit of a monster undertaking.'' This last bit was said as much to Ellie as to Abby, and Ellie tilted her head back and smiled up at him. He tightened his arms around his bride-to-be, and Abby got the distinct impression that the entire diner could disappear and Parker Monroe wouldn't care, just as long as Ellie stayed. ''Everything going well, Abby?''

Abby nodded, but she couldn't help feeling a small ache, witnessing the happiness of the two couples in front of her. ''Griffin has contractors coming in to begin on the basketball courts and the football field today, and I have all the gardens mapped out. I plan to plant most of the flowers myself, but I'll turn the bigger plots over to the high school kids I've hired for the summer. Everything's well organized and under control,'' she said, careful not to sound too defiant, hoping no one could tell how her emotions churned just at the mention of Griffin's name.

''Griffin must be pleased, then,'' Parker said. ''This project is very important to him.''

''I hope everything works out,'' Ellie said worriedly. ''I'm afraid I had a part in convincing him that Red

Rose would be good for his little boy. I hope I was right.''

''Casey already seems to love the house, and he's excited at being with Griffin,'' Abby offered. But she understood what Ellie meant. Griffin's child meant everything to him. She would never want to be responsible for bringing sorrow into that relationship. Nor would she want to bring pain into any child's life. And for the first time, Abby admitted just how terrified she was of giving birth. Soon she would be just as responsible for a child as Griffin was. She would have to be very careful of what she did and said.

''Come on, love. We've got things to do,'' Chester said, giving Sunny's fanny a pat.

''Don't do that,'' Sunny said, but then she practically purred as she took the hand he was holding out to her. ''At least don't do it here.''

And suddenly Abby felt as if she were suffocating. She really wasn't sure she could do the couples scene. Like Sunny, she had always been a hell-bent-for-leather kind of woman, self-sufficient and proud of it. Having some man turn her into a melting chocolate drop was just too much to imagine…or to endure. In truth, she didn't think there was a man on earth who could touch her and make her look as heated as Sunny looked.

And against her will, an image of herself plastered against Griffin's bare chest rose up. She slammed it away as she rose from the table in a rush. Her head whirled and swam and she nearly had to sit down again.

''Abby?'' Parker asked gently. ''Are you all right?''

She tried to nod.

''Let's get her home,'' he said to Ellie.

Abby held out her hand. ''No, I've got work to do.''

Ellie shook her head. ''Griffin is an understanding

man, Abby. Just let me call him and tell him you're not well, and then we'll go."

For some reason, Abby just couldn't deal with that. A vision of Griffin carrying his son so gently the day before filled her mind. She had a terrible feeling that he would want to comfort her in some way, too, that he was one of those men who were solicitous defenders and protectors of women. And if he showed up being solicitous, he might touch her. And she might…

She sat down, hard. She worked at summoning up a no-nonsense, stern look, which she turned on Ellie and Parker.

"I am completely fine," she said. "I just stood up too quickly. It's perfectly normal," she insisted. "Thank you, but don't even think about calling Griffin. I'm just going to finish my coffee, and then I'm going to get up slowly and go about my business as usual. Please," she said when they looked uncertain. "It's important to me that I be able to maintain some sense of normalcy during my pregnancy. So much of being pregnant makes me feel crazy and out of control. I at least want to be able to maintain control where my business is concerned."

Reluctantly Parker nodded. Ellie frowned, but when Parker touched her hand, she took a breath. "All right, but you have to agree to call if anything happens."

"If you can't get Ellie or Parker, you can call me," Delia said. "Let me give you my brand-new cell phone number."

At that, a chorus of yesses circled the room, and soon Abby was holding a small stack of phone numbers on scraps of paper, even though she already knew most of the numbers by heart.

A lump started to form in her throat as she looked

around at the usual Red Rose crowd. "You guys are the best," she said. They were all she needed. She certainly didn't need any man. But then she shifted on her seat and felt her small but growing abdomen. She did need a man, and the only one she had been near lately was making her crazy with the longing to touch him.

Darn it all. She needed to extricate Griffin from her thoughts, but how?

She knew what Sunny would say. The best way to forget a man was to replace him with another. The sooner that happened the better she and her child would be. So what in the world was taking Thomasina so long?

"All right, I think I have someone who might work," Thomasina said, when Abby called her several hours later. "I wanted to interview him further to make sure, but maybe I'm being too thorough, taking the mystery out of the process. It's probably best for you and Haydn to simply meet and begin on your journey of discovery."

Okay, she couldn't let this one pass. "Journey of discovery?"

"Getting to know each other," Thomasina clarified.

"That's better," Abby agreed. "I want to keep this simple."

She thought she heard Thomasina sigh, but she couldn't be sure about that. And soon enough Thomasina had turned all-business and agreed to set up the particulars of Abby's first date for tomorrow night. At Abby's insistence, Thomasina arranged for Haydn to meet Abby at a restaurant two towns over.

No way do I want any of my friends observing this, Abby thought. She realized that her palms were perspiring and her stomach was churning. Her heart was doing funny flippy things, too. She needed distraction, and for her that always meant work. So she was on her knees two hours later when Griffin located her.

"Hi. Where's Casey?" she asked, looking up from the lilac bush she was planting.

Her question brought a smile to his face. "Wheedling his way into the cook's heart. I think she's pulling out all of her cookbooks, and Case is putting in his order."

She could just picture the little boy pointing to the pictures of the things he liked best. Mrs. Digner would no doubt bend over backward to please him. He was so sweet and spontaneous.

"Nice smile, but it's a bit weary. You need a break," Griffin told her, holding out his hand. His clean hand. How come she always had dirt all over her whenever she met this man?

Maybe because she spent her life wallowing in the stuff? And he knew that?

She placed her hand in his, readying herself for the kick of his touch. She wasn't disappointed. Her heart reacted just as she'd known it would. Her respiration rose to near visible levels and didn't return to normal when she was back on her feet and no longer touching Griffin.

"I'm really fine." She just had to say it. It wasn't in her nature to plead fatigue or helplessness.

"I heard you nearly fainted in the Red Rose today."

"When did you hear that? Or maybe I should ask who told you?"

He shrugged. "I just got off the phone with Parker."

She placed her hands on her hips as she frowned up at him. "I wouldn't have thought Parker was a tattle-tale."

"Abby..."

She blushed. "I know. Don't say it. He's a wonderful man, a really good guy, and I know he was just doing the gentlemanly thing, but..."

"But you don't like me to treat you with any deference to your condition."

"It's not that." Although it was, a little. "I'm going to have a baby, and maybe I'm going to have it alone. I have to be a strong person."

"Taking a rest now and then doesn't make you a weak one. It's just the right thing to do."

"But if people see me struggling, they'll want to help me all the time."

"Is that so bad?"

Only if you were the kind of person who had grown up counting only on yourself.

"I just don't want to become dependent on others. It's the way I like things, and it's wiser to be that way." Because others could walk away, they could fail you; they might end up being weak and letting you down.

"Abby, people care about you. They want to help. Do you realize that, in the past week, I've been warned by no less than twenty people about what would happen if I did anything to hurt you?"

She thought she was going to be sick at first, but then, because she was who she was, she caught herself. Anger and indignation won out, thank goodness.

"Who dared to say that to you?" How utterly humiliating, especially when she thought about what it implied, that Griffin would either talk her into his bed or talk his way into her heart. As if he would want to try and she would be willing to let him.

Forcefully she pushed away the memories of how her wickedly willing body reacted every time he touched her.

"Abby, I wasn't mentioning this to complain."

"You should be. It's insulting to you."

"No, it's not. These are your friends, and I only told you about the warnings so you'd know how very much they adore you. These are the kind of people you can trust. You should trust them and let them help you when they can. It will make them feel better."

"It will?"

He smiled a long, slow smile, and her heart started doing that crazy free fall it did whenever she accidentally brushed against him. "Definitely," he agreed. "And I'll feel much better if you let me make a few concessions to your condition, too. You're doing a wonderful job here," he said, motioning toward the new plantings that were sprouting up everywhere. "You're probably well ahead of schedule. So please, take it easy on your body and don't try to do too much at once. Let your crew do more. Let me fuss a little. I'm going to worry if you don't either voluntarily take more frequent rest periods or at least let me show up and order you to take a breather now and then."

It would have to be voluntary, she thought. When he did this to her, when he touched her and smiled at her, she felt great waves of longing well up in her. Couldn't have that.

"All right," she agreed. "I'll try to remember to rest now and then."

"And put your feet up at night," he said. "Tonight you go home early and you do nothing."

She started to agree, but then she remembered and frowned.

"You're going to be difficult about this, aren't you, Abby?" Griffin asked, shaking his head. "You're a stubborn, stubborn woman."

"I know, but this time—" she held out her hands "—I have a date."

His gaze never left her. "One of Thomasina's men or one who simply followed you home?"

Abby blinked. "I'm not the kind of woman that men follow home."

He frowned, started to open his mouth, then frowned some more. "So Thomasina has set this up. Let's talk." And without waiting for her to respond, he took her hand and drew her to a new oak bench beneath a tree that had been planted just yesterday.

"Tell me," he said.

"There's nothing to tell. His name is Haydn Winrow, he's a farmer, and I'm meeting him at the Skyview Inn at seven o'clock."

"An inn?"

"It's a restaurant."

"Posh or cozy? Dark? Romantic?"

He was studying her closely. Asking her questions she hadn't really thought about.

"I don't remember exactly. Not romantic. This isn't that kind of date. And the Skyview...well, it's just a restaurant. I didn't want him to pick me up."

"Good girl."

She raised her chin. "Griffin, the man is not going to jump me."

"You don't know that."

"Thomasina knows him."

"Thomasina is a babe in the woods where men are concerned." Abby had the feeling that he wanted to add that she was, too. Well, he would have been wrong about that. She might not know much, but she was plenty cautious.

"So...are you excited?" he asked suddenly.

And the walls she'd built fell away. "I'm nervous," she confessed.

"Why?" The word was hard, like stone hitting stone.

She shrugged. "I don't know. Fear of the unknown, I guess."

"If he tries anything…"

She held up her hand. "I told you, he won't. It's just that nervousness of knowing that we both went to Thomasina to set this up. We both have a plan. I know what mine is."

He didn't answer. She looked up and saw that his eyes were angry. She could tell that he thought he knew what Haydn's plan was.

"He must know that I'm pregnant," she reminded him. "Thomasina would have been honest about that. Most likely he's just looking for a family. That's what I want."

"Well then, I hope that's what you get." Griffin's words were soft, his tone deep. "You should have what you want and need. Absolutely."

His last words were low, a whisper. Need rose up in Abby, and she had a painful fear that Haydn Winrow would never be able to supply what she wanted and needed, because what she wanted right this minute was for Griffin to cover her body with his, to kiss her until her lips were swollen.

What on earth was she going to do about that?

Chapter Six

Griffin stared down into Abby's lost blue eyes. And then she squared her shoulders as if she were preparing to march into battle or do something equally demanding. She twisted those pretty pink lips into a forced smile that still made his breath trip faster. "Let's go see what goodies Casey has talked Mrs. Digner into making," she said.

He got the picture. No more grilling her over her impending date. No more playing the Neanderthal, I'm-going-to-protect-you male. Well, all right, he'd done the wrong thing.

Too bad. It wasn't the first time he'd done the wrong thing with a woman, or even the hundredth. And this time he wasn't sorry. Abby was seriously desirable, and he couldn't feel good about this dangerous matchmaking enterprise she was setting out on. Strange men were not to be trusted.

Still, he dropped the subject.

"All right, let's do it," he said softly, and for a second she froze. "Let's go check out the kitchen," he clarified, and she relaxed once again. He didn't take her hand. It always seemed to make her jump. Made him jump, too. It also made him think of making love to her here in the green grass surrounded by all those plants she loved to whisper to.

He wanted her to whisper to him. Soft things. Urgent things. He wanted her to ask him to touch her.

Not that she would, but a man could fantasize, couldn't he?

Yeah, and that was all he could do. Abby needed a husband, a man to father that baby, not a man to do what her baby's father had done, have her and run out on her. He nearly groaned at the thought that he might even consider treating her the way that jerk had.

"Oh my," she said, and Griffin halted his errant thoughts and looked up.

He chuckled. Casey and Mrs. Digner were at the kitchen table. Casey's face and hands were liberally speckled with chocolate. The ordinarily spotless Mrs. Digner had a swirl of chocolate on her cheek. She blushed when she saw that she and Casey had an audience. And then she laughed.

"I haven't had so much fun baking in years," she confessed.

Griffin grinned at Abby, and then he threw caution to the wind and placed his hand against the small of her back, drawing her to the table. "Come on, we're missing all the good stuff," he told her.

To his delight, she played along. She laughed. "Can we share?" she asked Casey. "Is there enough?"

"Lots," he said, his big eyes lighting up. "Cookies in there, Dad," he said, pointing to the oven. "Mrs. Dig drawed names. Yours, too, Abby," he told her. "I had her draw a fwower one for you, too. A baseball one for Dad. One for Mom, too,'' he added. ''Okay?''

Griffin felt as if his knees would buckle, Casey's voice was so worried. Griffin's hand suddenly clenched against Abby's back, and half-afraid he'd hurt her, he moved away.

''You miss Mom, don't you?'' he asked.

Casey chewed at his lip, a worried look on his little face.

''It's all right to miss her, Case,'' Griffin said. ''And of course you can make her a cookie. As many as you want.''

Casey nodded solemnly. ''Miss you, too.''

''I'm here now.''

''Yep.'' But what was unsaid was clear. He wasn't always here. He had never always been around, and now he never could be.

Casey was swallowing hard, and suddenly Abby dropped to her knees beside him. ''Let's look at those neat cookies,'' she said. ''I really can't wait, but I bet if Mrs. Digner turns on the oven light we can watch them turn brown. It's like…it's just like watching them come to life. And you can tell your mom all about it later tonight when you call her. She is going to be so completely proud of you. It's not everyone who can make cookies, you know. I can't. In fact, I don't think I've ever made a cookie in my life.''

The lost look in Casey's eyes was replaced by surprise. ''But…Dad tode me you wuz gonna be a mommy.''

Abby tossed Griffin a look. Uh-oh, he thought. He probably should have asked her permission before he revealed her pregnant state to his son, but Casey was such a bundle of energy, Griffin had wanted him to know that they had to take a little care with Abby, that she was a bit more fragile than usual now.

"Yes, I'm going to be a mom," she said out loud, and her voice trembled over the word, as if she'd never said it, never even allowed herself to think it yet. Griffin knew something of what she felt. It had taken him a while to match up the word *dad* with his own image of himself. "Guess I'll have to learn how to make cookies, won't I? Maybe you can help teach me."

Casey grinned and clenched a cookie that was starting to crumble in his tight grip. "I'm a good cookie guy."

"The best," Mrs. Digner agreed. "He was very specific about what he wanted on each cookie. He's very good with details."

Just as I was, Griffin thought. The thought brought a pang to his heart. He hoped his son wasn't going to be just like him. He was proud of many of his accomplishments, maybe even most of them. He was content with his life, but there were parts of his life he hoped his son would get to avoid.

Like not getting to see his child every day when he woke up. Like missing many of the milestones in his son's life, because they lived in different places.

"Griffin?"

Griffin looked down and saw that Abby was staring at him, concern deepening the blue of her eyes.

"Let's look at those cookies," he said, forcing a hearty tone to his voice.

To his dismay, she didn't look away and she didn't look convinced. But then he motioned slightly toward Casey, and she nodded and pasted a smile on. "What's that?" she asked, pointing to a cookie that looked a bit like a snowman whose bottom had been switched to his middle.

"You," Casey said, shaking his head incredulously. "Mrs. Dig says ladies growing babies get fat. When will you be?"

Abby choked a bit. Griffin grinned, reached out and patted her on the back. "Yes, when will you be fat, Abby?" he asked.

She gave him a warning glare, then turned to smile at Casey. "I think…soon. The baby is starting to grow bigger already," she told him.

"Good. I like babies. Can I pet him when he comes?"

Mrs. Digner started to chuckle, but Abby slid closer to the little boy. "He won't be here for a long time still, Casey," she said quietly.

"Oh." The sound rang hollow. Even at four Casey knew that he would be back home before a long time passed.

"But you can help me think of some good names for him," she promised. "I haven't decided on one yet."

Casey's frown turned to a sun-bright smile. "Dooney," he said. "I like Dooney."

Abby blinked.

"Dooney is Casey's turtle," Griffin explained.

"I like Dooney," Casey said again.

"Well, I'll certainly put it on the list," Abby agreed, as Mrs. Digner hid a smile behind her hand and busied herself taking the hot cookies out of the oven. Just then the clock chimed.

Abby looked up, and a slightly panicked look turned her eyes dark. "Oh, I didn't realize it was this late. I have to be going," she said. "I'm sorry."

Casey looked stricken. ''You ain't had your cookie yet.''

Griffin touched his son's cheek. ''Maybe Abby could take her cookie with her. She has a date,'' he explained.

''A date?''

''Yes, she's meeting...a friend. A man.'' The words sounded wrong in Griffin's ears.

''Man? Like you?''

''No,'' Abby said suddenly, and Griffin felt a small shaft of anger slide through him. The lady certainly didn't want anything to do with him. But when he looked at her, she blushed, and he remembered the taste of her and how her body had molded against his. The lady didn't want to like him, but she did. A little. At least her body responded to his, even if she didn't want it to.

Somehow that didn't make him feel much better. She was still set on meeting a total stranger at an inn.

Casey looked confused, worried. ''Don't you like Dad?''

Abby's eyes grew wide. She opened her mouth and nothing came out at first. ''It's not that,'' she finally said. ''It's just...I—''

''When Abby said that her date wasn't like me, she meant that Mr. Winrow lives around here,'' Griffin explained. ''Not like me.''

She cast him a grateful look. ''Mr. Winrow is a farmer,'' she explained.

''You like farmers?''

''I suppose I do, if they're nice.''

''Mommy says I'm nice.''

''You are, sweetie. You're the nicest.''

''You like me better than the farmer.''

It wasn't a question, Griffin thought. More like an order. How simple to be a child and state your wishes.

But not simple at all really, he reminded himself. All too often a child's wishes didn't come into play.

"I'm sure I couldn't like him better than you," Abby said softly. "He'd have to be super extra special, and that doesn't happen very often."

"Dad's super extra," Casey said.

Abby smiled weakly. "Do you think the cookies are cool enough to try?" she asked, changing the subject. And without waiting for an answer, she scooped up the one decorated with flowers. "It's almost too pretty to eat," she told Casey.

"You can eat it," he said. "Yes. Now."

She did. Griffin could tell that her mouth was burning, at least a little.

"It's yummy," she said, after she'd swallowed a mouthful. "The best."

"Take one to the farm man," Casey offered. "This one," he said, pointing to one that was more than a bit misshapen and a little burned on the edge.

"Thank you, sweetie. I will," Abby said. And she got to her feet, wrapped the cookie in a napkin, told Casey and Mrs. Digner goodbye and turned to Griffin.

"I'll walk you to your truck," he offered.

"That's okay. You don't have to."

"Maybe I have business to talk about."

Her brow furrowed with disbelief, but she nodded and moved ahead of him out the door.

"I've almost finished the flower beds between the baseball and soccer fields," she said. "I'm going to start on the cherry trees east of the basketball courts. Is there something you want changed?"

Yes. He wanted her to break ties with her matchmaker.

''The flowers are beautiful. I'm happy with the job so far. Just make sure you take a cell phone with you tonight. Don't leave it in your car the way you do sometimes when you're here. Call me if you need anything or if anything seems wrong or just different than you would want it to.''

She opened her mouth to argue, but then she nodded. ''Thank you, but I'll be fine, Griffin.''

That wasn't the answer he wanted. ''Men can be jerks sometimes,'' he said. As if she didn't know that. Hadn't her baby's father already taught her that?

''Are you talking in general terms or are you talking about yourself?'' she asked suddenly.

''Both,'' he agreed.

''You're not a jerk.''

''I have been. I wasn't a good husband, Abby. There's a reason I don't have Casey all the time.''

''You're not telling me you were abusive to your wife?''

He sucked in a breath. ''I would never hurt a woman, whether I loved that woman or not, but a man can be deficient in other ways. He can be uncaring. He can simply be all wrong for the woman. Don't stay if you think he's all wrong for you, Abby. Don't get caught.''

She raised her chin. ''I'm a strong woman, Griffin.''

''I know.''

But someone had obviously caught her off guard at one time.

''I'll make you one promise,'' she said. ''If I feel I can't handle the situation, I'll call you.''

And he guessed he would just have to be satisfied

with that. ''All right,'' he agreed, as she climbed in her truck and prepared to drive away. Just before she did, she rolled down the window.

''What did you do that made you…not right for her?'' she asked.

He looked her straight in the eye. ''I left her alone for long periods of time. I neglected her and my son. I was never there when she needed me. I didn't love her,'' he admitted, to her and to himself.

When he said the words out loud, it made him sound a lot like the man who had left Abby alone and pregnant. His voice sounded hollow. Suddenly he felt hollow.

''I'm sorry I asked,'' she said. ''I was feeling defensive and trying to prove I wouldn't back away from any situation, no matter how touchy, but it wasn't really any of my business,'' she said softly. ''Forgive me for prying.''

''You needed to know the truth,'' he said. And he needed to let her know. If they were to be together and not give in to the desire that shimmered between them, he needed to be honest and open.

And watching her drive away to an unknown fate, Griffin realized there was one more thing he needed to do, as well. If he asked Abby, or even Thomasina, they would tell him it was the wrong thing to do. No doubt it was, but somehow he just didn't care. If he didn't do something, he was going to seriously worry about Abby.

And if anything happened to her and he hadn't done all he could to protect her, how was he going to feel about that?

Exactly.

He would have liked to dog Abby's steps to watch over her, but catching sight of him would put a serious crimp in her plans, and he had no right to do that. Moreover, he wasn't certain he could sit still and watch while Haydn Winrow courted her, even if he didn't try anything that would get his nose smashed.

No, that just wasn't going to work. What would?

With a whoosh of breath and a large dose of resignation, Griffin picked up the telephone. He made a few calls, set some wheels in motion. He considered the fact that if Abby got wind of this, there was going to be some serious hell to pay. One way or another his actions were certainly going to rub her the wrong way, maybe even hurt her feelings. Once again he was handling a woman all wrong.

For two seconds he thought about doing what most men would have done and calling things off completely. But when the two seconds had passed, he remembered what a trusting creature Thomasina was, and it was Thomasina who had set this up. Haydn Winrow could be a dope, he could be a good guy, or he could be a man looking to take advantage of a woman in need. He might even have the bad sense and the gall to think that because Abby had gone to a matchmaker that gave him the right to skip a few steps in the courtship process and get right to some serious pawing.

A low growl slipped through Griffin's lips. No woman deserved that, but especially not Abby. She had jumped right in to make Casey smile, she talked to flowers and trees, she was brave and sweet and all on her own. He hated knowing that.

And he knew then and there that no matter how much this damaged his relationship with Abby, he was bound and determined to interfere.

* * *

"I've got a good-size farm and three babies," Haydn Winrow said, staring at Abby, a question in his eyes. "My ex-wife didn't want anything to do with either the farm or the kids, and she left us high and dry."

Abby felt a sense of unease. She looked away from the man's angry brown eyes. She couldn't fault him for laying his cards on the table. If she had a farm to work and three children, she'd be anxious, too. But the pressure that had been chasing her for weeks intensified at his words.

"Do you like farming?" she asked.

"It's what I do," he said simply. "Ms. Edgerton tells me you own a flower shop."

"I do, but I have an assistant who handles most of that part of the business. I do landscaping when I can. This summer I've been lucky enough to land my favorite type of job."

"With the billionaire from Chicago I've heard about."

"What have you heard?"

"Not much. That he's filthy rich, that the women like him, that he'll head back to the city and take his money with him come fall."

Well, he had certainly nailed that one, Abby thought. She shifted on her seat and looked off to the side.

"It's a good job. He's a fair employer," she said a bit defensively, trying to hold back her blush of embarrassment and anger.

"Sorry," Haydn said, and he reached across the table to take her fingers, a move that made her feel vaguely uncomfortable, like mild morning sickness. For a moment she thought she saw a sixtyish bearded man a few tables down eyeing her and Haydn. For just a second it looked as if that man might be looking at her hand in

Haydn's. The bearded man shifted in his chair, as if he was going to get up.

Just then, Haydn stroked her fingers, and she pulled them away. The bearded man returned to his coffee and pie.

"I'm...I thought we were just going to meet tonight," she said.

Haydn nodded. "Guess I jumped the gun. Tell me more about your job."

Abby nodded, grateful for something easy to talk about. "Griffin's got good ideas. You wouldn't think a baseball field could look like anything but a baseball field, but his looks like... I don't know...a place where some young Little Leaguer's dreams could come true. Perfect grass, lots of lights, a great view beyond the field. And the dugout is pure luxury. He said that he bases all his products on the kinds of things he used to want when he was growing up."

Her date was eyeing her, a question in his eyes. "Sounds like the man can have anything he wants right now."

Uh-oh. A man whose wife had left him for the finer things in life wouldn't want to hear about Griffin. Still, an image of Griffin and Casey helping her dig in the dirt rose up.

"He's a good man. He's not obnoxious about his wealth," she said.

"I'll bet it's easy to be nice when you have money," the man answered.

And from there on out, things just went downhill. At one point Abby looked up and her eyes met those of the bearded man. He looked strangely sympathetic. And when she and Haydn left, he followed them out. She should have been alarmed. Somehow she wasn't.

She paid her half of the dinner and tried to thank Haydn for the evening, but he only shook his head at her. Abby had a feeling he was going to have a thing or two to say to Tommy.

As she got in her car and started the engine, she looked up and saw the bearded man watching her. He smiled and saluted her, then drove off in front of her.

What a strange and uncomfortable evening. She wondered how Griffin and Casey had spent these past few hours. She wondered if Griffin ever dated, and if he ever introduced his dates to his son.

She was pretty sure that if Griffin ever got to that stage with a woman, his date wouldn't end up wondering why things had gone so badly. No doubt the lady would end the evening smiling.

Especially if Griffin took her in his arms and kissed her.

Abby hit the accelerator too hard as the thought of Griffin's lips on hers sent desire shooting through her.

''No more,'' she told herself, getting the car under control. Still, she couldn't deny the fact that when Haydn had stroked her fingers, she had wanted to pull away, but when Griffin had touched his lips to hers, she'd wanted to slip her hands beneath his shirt and feel his naked skin warm against her fingertips.

Life was darn unjust and senseless at times.

And who in heck was that bearded man?

Chapter Seven

"Is she all right?" Griffin asked the man on the other end of the line.

"Perfectly fine. He didn't do much."

"What does that mean exactly?" Griffin practically barked the words into the phone.

"It means she was handling herself just fine."

Which meant that Griffin was probably over the line, sending a bodyguard to watch over Abby.

"Do you want the whole story? Some of my clients want all the details. What she wore. What he wore. How she looked. What they said. How much touching went on, how much laughing, what kind of car he drove, whether she looked like she was enjoying herself..."

Griffin felt a bit sick at the thought that he had paid someone to invade Abby's personal life to this extent. "If she's all right, that's all I need to know."

"I can take pictures next time if you like," Nick Sevren offered.

Something like a chill ran through Griffin. "No.

What you've given me is sufficient. Don't do more. In fact, if there's a next time, don't go near unless you absolutely have to. Only if he tries to harm her or take advantage in a way that frightens her."

"And then?"

"Get her away from him."

"Your call, Mr. O'Dell. You're in control."

And that was a falsehood if ever he'd heard one, Griffin thought, because just then he looked up and saw Abby's blue truck coming down the road. His pulse started to pound, testosterone flowed through his body.

Yeah, he was in control all right. Like Pavlov's dogs, all he had to do was see the woman and he started to salivate.

Abby climbed out of her truck and gazed toward the house, which was surrounded by several crews of workers, all transforming the formerly empty green fields into a class-A sports complex. Griffin had just come outside, and he waved to her but didn't come near. Instead, he headed toward a big O'Dell Sporting Goods truck that had pulled up in the yard.

A touch of disappointment slipped through her, but she quickly brushed it aside. Obviously, the man had work to do. He couldn't spend all his time talking to her.

She busied herself supervising the two teenagers she had hired to dig the koi pond. But it was hard to concentrate when she could hear the sounds of Casey's laughter.

"Up, Dad. Whee!"

Okay, it was impossible to concentrate. Abby turned in time to see Casey sitting on Griffin's shoulders, a miniature basketball clutched in his hands as Griffin moved beneath the basket to give his son a fighting chance to toss the ball in.

Casey launched the basketball, which missed the basket by a long shot and nearly thunked Griffin in the head.

"That was close, Case. Nearly a basket," he said, and Abby smiled at the whopper of a lie. No question, Casey would never suffer from low self-esteem if it was up to his father "You want to try again, Sport, or do you want to go see what else came in on the truck?"

"The truck!" Casey said. "Bill tode me I could see in."

"And Bill is a man of his word if ever I met one," Griffin said with a laugh.

He turned at that moment, and his eyes met Abby's. It almost felt as if he captured her with his glance. She couldn't move, couldn't breathe for a moment as his assessing silver gaze slid over her. As if she might have changed somehow from last night to this morning.

She had half an urge to rush to a mirror to see what Griffin saw. What made his eyes go dark like that? Of course, now that he'd caught her staring at him, there was no way she could try to lie and pretend that she hadn't been watching, so she shrugged and slowly began making her way toward them.

"Abby, I'm goin' in the truck," Casey declared, and he disappeared behind the big truck where two tanned arms reached down and lifted him inside.

She smiled. "The thrill of discovery?" she asked as she drew near to Griffin.

"Not much that can beat it. New stuff is always fun."

"I have a feeling *this* new stuff is better than most."

"I try. So...how was *your* new stuff?"

She frowned in confusion.

"The new man," he clarified. "The date."

"Oh." Abby looked away. "It was just a first date."

"Meaning that there will be a second one?"

"No! That is...it didn't go all that well."

"You didn't like him?"

"He didn't like me."

Griffin frowned. "So the man has gravel for brains, then?"

Abby smiled in spite of herself. "No, he's just had a bad experience with a woman. He wants a wife who's completely devoted to him, and...well, I'm afraid I bored him. I made the mistake of mentioning my boss. He sure didn't like you much."

Griffin tilted his head and gave her a sexy smile. "Maybe he's territorial, and he views any male as a competitor for his woman's attention."

She tried hard to breathe normally. "Well, I hardly think so, but still, I guess I was wrong to go on a date with one man and talk about work and my boss so much. He didn't seem to think I could be satisfied with a mere farmer."

"Could you?"

"I don't know."

"Did you want to see him again?"

Abby hesitated. She had the distinct feeling that if she said yes, Griffin would try to buy Haydn for her. "No. To be honest, he kind of scared me a little."

"Abby." The word sounded as if it was wrenched from him, and he moved right up into her space. "He didn't do anything."

It wasn't a question, more like a command.

"No, of course not, and I could have handled him if he had. He was just angry about women in general, especially women who had associations with well-to-do men.''

''Is that what we have? An association?'' She looked up into his eyes. There was a teasing smile on his lips, but his eyes were intense.

She didn't know what they had. All she knew was that when she was this near to him she couldn't think straight at all, and that scared the socks right off of her. It made her vulnerable in a way she never wanted to be again.

Slowly she nodded. ''I think so. You're my boss. I'm your employee. That makes this an association. Doesn't it?''

''I suppose you could make a case for that. But back to the farmer. He didn't touch you, but he scared you. Did he say anything that offended you? If he did...'' Griffin stepped closer as if he would protect her from cutting words with his very body. If she reached out right now, she could easily lean into him and graze her fingertips across his chest. Abby swallowed again. She tried to speak but couldn't find her voice.

''He didn't hurt me. I was okay.'' Her voice came out a strangled whisper.

''You were okay last night. How about now that you've had some time to think?''

Griffin dipped his head as if to catch her next words. He reached out and touched her cheek.

Abby's heart stopped beating and then it started up again twice as fast as it should be. ''I—'' She didn't have a clue what she meant to say...or even what he had asked. All she knew was that he was close enough to kiss, and she wanted to kiss him. Terribly.

''Abby?'' Griffin slid his fingers into her hair. She closed her eyes and savored the sensation.

"Abby," he repeated, and this time the word was a caress. He was going to kiss her.

She was going to enjoy it, savor it, want more of him, and when the summer ended and he left, what would she have?

Quickly she shook her head. She tried to smile, even though her lips were trembling and the smile wouldn't quite stick.

"I'm fine. Really. It was a nothing date. I wasn't hurt in any way. I wasn't offended." She reached up to catch his hand and pull away, but then she realized that touching his hand might intensify the feeling.

He studied her, carefully, intently. Then he gave a tight nod and pulled his hand away. He took a step back.

"Good. No harm done, then."

Was he talking about her date or about the past few moments? She couldn't stand the thought of him knowing that she could be affected by him, especially when she knew he already felt that he'd failed his wife.

"Absolutely no harm done," she said to reassure him, no matter what he had meant.

"Dad, Dad! What's this?"

Was that relief on Griffin's face? It certainly was what *she* was feeling. Saved by a child. How fitting. How right.

Abby touched her abdomen. She couldn't seem to help it these days, making that connection.

Griffin smiled. "Be right there, Case. Tell him hello for me," he whispered to Abby.

"Casey?" she asked.

"The baby."

She frowned, confused.

"Abby, you talk to plants, you talk to the ground we walk on. You can't tell me you don't talk to your little one.'' And he smiled and turned toward his own little one.

Well, he had caught her on that one. She hadn't yet spoken to the baby, even though she knew that many women did. And Abby admitted to herself right then that she was more afraid than she'd known. It was one thing to touch her stomach, the evidence that life would never be the same. It was something completely different to make a connection to the child growing within her, to talk to her baby as if it was already a part of her life. The child she and she alone was responsible for.

The sudden reality startled her, scared her to death. Her knees nearly buckled beneath the weight of the truth as it grew within her and grew stronger. She really was responsible for this baby. Not down the road, not when he or she was born. Now and forever. How her baby lived and breathed, survived, grew up, grew happy and grew older was entirely up to her. Or at least up to her and God, but she had a strong feeling that God expected her to do her fair share of the work. He wouldn't have given this child to her to raise otherwise. But was she up to it? And what if she didn't find a father? Was it fair to her baby to let her start life without a father?

Fathers were important, she thought as she watched Griffin lift Casey high in his arms and hug him close before spinning him around. Of course, she'd already known that. Children who grew up without fathers in a world filled with them knew they were missing something big. She didn't want her baby to miss the kinds of things that Griffin gave to his child.

''Again, Dad,'' Casey yelled. ''Higher.''

Yes, fathers were really important.

''Abby, see me. I'm big,'' Casey called, looking down from his high perch.

And she left her thoughts behind and wandered over to the beautiful man and boy. ''You are one very tall guy,'' she agreed. ''I feel positively tiny next to you.''

He beamed at her. ''My fader lifted me here,'' he said. ''My fader can do anything.''

Her heart hurt.

''He probably can,'' she agreed. ''I've heard he has magic in his fingertips.''

''He can fro a ball and he can hit one hard. He's got muscles. Feel.'' Casey reached down and touched his father's arm. He waited for Abby to do the same.

Griffin grinned slyly as she hesitated. ''Yes, Abby, feel,'' he said.

Still she hesitated.

''I don't think she believes I'm as strong as you say,'' he told Casey.

And Casey reached out. Abby did the only thing she could do. She put her hand in his and he guided it to Griffin's biceps. Her fingers barely grazed his skin, but she thought she saw his chest rise. Hers didn't, but that was only because she was holding her breath to keep him from seeing her reaction.

''You were right,'' she told Casey as she quickly slipped her hand back into her pocket and avoided looking into Griffin's eyes. ''Your father is very strong.''

''A man could certainly get used to all this praise,'' Griffin said with a chuckle, and she couldn't help it then. She laughed, too. Casey, in the way of little children who followed their elders' leads, laughed along.

Just then Abby heard a whir and a click. She turned to see Bob Davies, a reporter for the local newspaper, lowering his camera.

"Hey, Ab," he called. "I'm just doing a story on some of the new people in town and how it's livening things up around here and bringing new business to old merchants. Not that you're old," he explained, "but everybody knows that Mr. O'Dell hired you to do a pretty big job. Isn't this something?" he asked, turning in a circle and snapping off picture after picture of the new gardens and sports fields. "Looks like a completely different place from what I remember growing up. A lot better," he admitted. "What a showpiece. You don't mind if I print a few pictures of the progress in the paper, do you?" he asked Griffin.

Griffin shrugged. "What man would complain about free publicity?" But then he seemed to think of something. "But…they're your gardens, Abby. What do you think?"

She thought that Bob was a good reporter and said so. "My work here is pretty far along," she said. "I could use this for my portfolio to show prospective customers, and it might be something the rest of the people in town could use when they're trying to attract new businesses to Red Rose. Shoot away, Bob." And she laughed and did one of those runway poses. "Don't use that one, though," she said as he clicked the shutter. "My ego couldn't deal with the ribbing."

"I don't think ribbing is what you'd get," Griffin said. "More like men driving by your door every night to see if you're available."

"He's got you there," Bob said with a laugh. "You're still a hot babe for a pregnant woman." He and Griffin exchanged a look. "But don't tell my wife I said that. Jen is the jealous type."

Abby laughed. "She's a sweetie who loves you to death, and she cooks like an angel."

Bob winked. ''Yes, I'm lucky to have her. Let's snap a few more action shots, show me what you two have been doing here, and then I've got to get to town. I'm hoping to run this one this week.''

So for the next half hour, Bob took shots of Abby kneeling in the gardens with Griffin looking on, shots of Abby and Griffin and Casey gathered around the bush they had planted together, and one of all of them peering into the hole that would soon be the koi pond. When he asked Griffin to give him a demo at the horseshoe pit, Griffin glanced down at his son, who was beginning to look drowsy.

''I'll take him in,'' Abby said, and Griffin passed the sleepy child into her waiting arms. Casey tucked his head beneath her chin as if the space had been made for him, and she gathered his little body close and tried not to think about what it would be like when he and Griffin had gone.

''Let's get you inside,'' she whispered against his dark, silky little-boy hair.

In response, he nestled closer. One grubby little hand moved up to rest on her shoulder. She glanced at Griffin, who gazed at his son with adoration. ''Thank you,'' Griffin said, and her throat nearly closed up. He *was* a strong man, but this child was his weakness. His love for his son was so obvious, it hurt to think that he had to give him up for most of the year.

''I'll keep him safe,'' she promised.

''I never doubted it.'' And his tone was so intense that tears formed behind her eyes. She turned quickly and carried Casey away.

''I'll run the story this weekend,'' Bob called softly.

''I'll look forward to it,'' she said, and then she took Casey inside.

A short time later, as she was watching Casey sleeping in his bed, Griffin walked up next to her. He smiled and began to untie Casey's shoes.

"I was afraid I would wake him," she explained. "He looks so sweet and happy."

"Thank goodness," Griffin said. "I was afraid Cheryl and I had damaged him badly. But he's a gem. I hope he's bouncing back and that our divorce hasn't hurt him too much. Taking off his shoes is the least of my worries. He sleeps like a bear in hibernation." He smiled. "You couldn't wake him. Come back in an hour and he'll still be sleeping the deep sleep of the innocent."

"You've protected him," she said softly. "You're an excellent father."

His hands stilled. "I was away a lot when he was little. Business. I can't ignore it, but I could have worked around it. That's something I don't forgive myself for, but I don't intend to ever again let him suffer for my shortcomings."

"I don't know what it was like then," she said softly, "but for now, when you're with him, it's good, very good. He was young before. This is what he'll remember."

Griffin's hands stilled. He looked up at her. "Thank you. I need to believe that. If I ever did anything that would damage him in any way again, I couldn't forgive myself. I have to live my life more carefully than I used to."

She gave a curt nod. It was so close to what she'd been thinking herself, this awesome responsibility of being a parent.

"Being a parent must be difficult," she said.

He studied her. "You'll be good at it. You took him

right in your arms and you held him. He trusted you, he likes you. You're a natural.''

So was he, but he had chosen never to have another child. She could certainly understand why. The urge to glance down to where her baby lay was almost an ache. She wanted to promise her child that she would never hurt her, that she would never let anything bad happen to her. But of course that was an impossible promise.

Griffin clearly felt that he had damaged his child once. It must have been a terribly painful thing to admit. No wonder he never wanted to go there again.

''He hasn't misplaced his trust,'' she said softly. ''It's obvious that you would take a bullet to save him. What could you ever do that would hurt him?''

Chapter Eight

The story that ran in the *Red Rose Gazette* was funny and entertaining, with a color picture on the front and several more inside. The one that ran in the *Lindley Junction NewsNotes,* a privately published gossip-fest from a neighboring town, was not nearly so nice.

Griffin slammed the few sheets of poor quality newsprint down on the table. It was obvious that someone outside of Red Rose had heard that the billionaire CEO of O'Dell Sporting Goods had set up shop here. It was also obvious that whoever had commissioned this story, one of his competitors perhaps, had an agenda and had heard that Bob Davies was doing a story. The Lindley Junction story had run the day before the one in Red Rose.

It was a special edition, hastily published and poorly written. The pictures were grainy, taken from a distance. There was one of him all but pressing Abby to him, one of Abby feeling his muscle as Casey looked on, one of Abby doing her runway pose, and the story told a tale of how much time Abby had been spending at the O'Dell mansion and that she had frequently been seen disappearing inside the house.

This was a hatchet job, one Abby didn't deserve.

"Can't necessarily say the same about you, buddy," he told himself. "You want her, and have from the start. This more or less makes that clear to anyone who cares to look." As some people liked to say, the camera didn't lie but the story was pure fiction. It implied things that just weren't so. He might lust after Abby, but there was nothing going on between them and nothing that would be going on.

He hoped Abby didn't see a copy.

But it was obvious that she had when she rolled up in her truck. She hopped out, her eyes too bright, her step too jaunty.

"Good morning," she said crisply. "Lots to do. Have to get right to work."

"I'll insist on a retraction," he said. "I have the clout to do that."

She nodded curtly. "That would be good. Do you think it will make any difference?"

Honestly, he thought, no. Once a juicy story had been printed, no one ever seemed to want to read the truth.

"It will to us," he said. "You'll be okay here?"

She gave a tight nod.

"I—" He looked to the side. "Can you watch Casey? I don't really want him to witness what's going to happen between me and the guy who printed this."

She opened her eyes wide. "You're not going to hit anybody, are you?"

He managed a tired smile. "That's not how a man gets things done. Physical strength isn't necessary in these cases. But I've been told that I look rather frightening when I'm going full tilt. I don't want to scare my child.''

''I'll take him with me to choose the fish for the pond. If that's all right. Do you think he might like that?''

Griffin's throat hurt suddenly. ''I think you're going to be one wonderful mother. What kid wouldn't enjoy a chance to say he helped stock a pond?''

She managed a wan smile. ''Thank you. I needed to hear that.''

He turned to go.

''Griffin?''

Griffin turned and looked at her. She looked small and alone and terribly lovely. He waited for her to speak.

''The story— You haven't been to town much, what with all the work. I was hoping you'd let me take you in and introduce you around.''

''Because…?''

She blushed an endearing pink. ''Some people who don't know you believe that you may be taking advantage of me.''

He stared into her eyes. She didn't look away.

''Do you think that?'' he asked.

''No, of course not! But—''

''I don't usually pay much attention to what people say about me. Being a man with money causes people to talk.''

''I understand that, but Red Rose isn't a very big town. Everyone knows everyone else. Everyone cares.''

''And you think I should care.''

She raised her chin. ''I know how much it means to you to make Casey happy. I don't want people to think the worst of you, to have to risk having him hear untruths. If you came to town with me, people would see you for what you are. They're fair, Griffin. They know what that Lindley Junction rag is like. All they need is to talk to you a bit. Then they'll stand behind you no matter what happens."

"Are you telling me they would hurt my child?"

"Not intentionally, no. But they might feel sorry for him. They might reach out to him, and he might hear things he was never meant to hear. I'm just saying, let's show everyone that there's no reason at all to whisper. For Casey's sake."

"And we'll do that how?"

She looked to the side. "Just come for coffee. Tomorrow at the café. Everyone will be there."

"Because they've heard the rumors."

She frowned. "Because they're always there. It's where people go in the morning. It's community, family. My family."

His stern look softened. "I seem to remember that feeling from the first day, when I ventured into the café to find you. Well, all right then, Abby. I'd love to meet your family. Casey, too?"

She smiled, and some of the tension eased from around Griffin's heart. "Of course, Casey, too. He's going to be such a hit. Don't worry. We'll fix things. The people of Red Rose know the truth when it hits them between the eyes."

He gazed back at her. "If we're going to talk truth, then you and I should admit the whole truth."

She took a visible deep breath. "What do you mean?"

He took a step toward her, then stopped in midstride. "Abby, there's not a man alive who could look at that shot of me reaching for you and not realize that I wanted to make love to you right then and there. The truth is that I *do* desire you.''

She turned that luscious shade of rose again. It was all he could do not to take her in his arms. ''No one faults a man for feeling desire, Griffin. Any woman could see that I wanted you, too. Most of them wouldn't mind having you in their beds, for that matter.''

''So the truth is…that we want each other?''

She raised her chin. ''And also that we don't intend to do anything about it. Acting on our desires would be—''

''Incredibly risky. A mistake we couldn't undo,'' he said. ''You need a staying kind of man. I need to prove myself an honorable man for my son's sake. And maybe for my own sake.''

Abby nodded slowly. ''Yes, to all of that,'' she said softly.

''So you don't mind if people know that I find you desirable as long as they also know that that's as far as it goes?'' He couldn't help smiling at her brave front.

To his surprise, she smiled back, a lovely sight if he ever saw one. ''Well, it's actually kind of flattering to have such a handsome man telling people that he still finds me desirable. Us visibly pregnant women don't usually inspire that kind of reaction from a man.''

He looked down to where she had nested her hands over her belly. It was true. There was a slight bulge beneath her laced fingers.

He'd never seen anything so beautiful. A sudden urge to lift her top and kiss her on her bare skin raced through him.

''You are the sexiest woman on the planet,'' he told her, his voice rough, ''and anyone who says anything different is out of his ever-lovin' mind.''

And he winked at her.

She blinked and looked confused for a moment. Then, with a visible effort to cover up her reaction, she grinned at Griffin and wrinkled her nose. She glanced down at her stomach. ''Well, little Dooney, the day is looking decidedly more cheery. Time to go gather up my best beau, Casey, and see if we can catch some prizewinning show fish.'' And she laughed, waved goodbye to Griffin and turned on one heel to head toward the house. Her hips had a lovely, jaunty swing to them that was as much a part of her as her pretty red hair.

Griffin had no doubt that she would catch something this morning, or that she would net a wonderful husband very soon. It was all he could do to keep *his* heart from getting hooked.

Time to practice being strong. This time he intended to be smart where a woman was concerned. He was going to do the right thing if it killed him. He only hoped that newspaper story didn't hurt Abby or Casey. Once something was in black and white, the story seemed to grow and spread. No doubt the Chicago society pages would be carrying snippets from the *Lindley Junction NewsNotes* tomorrow.

The next day Abby entered the Red Rose Café clutching Casey's little hand with Griffin bringing up the rear. ''Hi, Lydia. Sunny. Delia,'' she said to the women sitting at the table closest to the door. ''Hello, everyone.'' She waved to the rest of the room.

''Hello, yourself, stranger. We haven't seen you for a few days,'' Joyce Hives said. ''We've missed you.'' But Abby noticed that her eyes were on Griffin. Not that she could blame her friend.

"You're looking really good, though," Mercy Granahan said, twisting her plump hands together.

"Happy," Rosellen January added. She stared so intently at Abby that Abby knew she was doing her best not to look at Griffin and ask the question everyone was apparently dying to ask, which was whether Griffin was responsible for her cheerful expression. The truth, though, was that her genial expression was hanging there by sheer determination.

"Good morning, Mr. O'Dell." Evangelina Purcell finally broke ranks and acknowledged Griffin's presence. "It's good to see you again." Broad-shouldered, mannish Evangelina was not a blushing woman, but she almost twittered when she looked at Griffin.

He winked at her and took the hand she was holding out, and for a minute Abby thought the stalwart woman just might faint.

But her words started a chorus of "Welcome, Mr. O'Dell," and Griffin ended up shaking lots of female hands.

"Abby, come on now, you can't keep that fine, handsome young man all to yourself. Introduce us, please," Sunny said, smiling at Casey after she'd pounded Griffin on the back and suggested he have a seat and a big cup of Lydia's coffee. "We haven't met him yet."

Abby gave Casey's hand a squeeze and looked down at him. He was looking a bit lost in the sea of women. "I was saving the best for last," she said. "This is Casey, everyone, and once you get to know him, you'll find out that he bakes a mean cookie. And he knows how to stock a pond."

"Well, those are definitely some pretty good things to know," Lydia said. "Pleased to meet you, Casey. And speaking of cookies, I just might have some in the kitchen. They're usually for the lunch crowd, but since this is your first time to the Red Rose, it's a kind of celebration. Would you like to go check it out? Would that be all right?"

Cookies, whoa, Abby thought, stealing a look at Griffin to see if he was going to nix the idea. After all, it was barely eight in the morning, but then, Lydia wasn't married and she didn't have any children, either.

Casey turned those big blue silver-dollar eyes on Lydia. "They chocolate?"

She smiled. "I'm sure some of them are."

He gazed up at his father, not asking the question.

Griffin wore a pained expression, but then he smiled. "All right, you've got me right where you want me. Go have some cookies, but no more than two. And ask Ms. Eunique for some milk or orange juice. At least you'll get some vitamins to go with your sugar."

Casey grinned. He turned to Lydia. "I like chocolate."

"Well then, we'll see what we can do," she said, and she took his hand and strolled off to the kitchen. "I'm kind of crazy for chocolate myself."

Abby knew what Lydia was doing. She was clearing a way for the serious talk to begin, and making sure that Casey didn't get hurt by any of it.

So, once the two of them had gone, silence set in...for about three seconds. Then Sunny turned those don't-dare-lie-to-me eyes on Griffin. "What on earth is going on out at the mansion?" she asked. "That newspaper article didn't look good."

Abby gritted her teeth. "Bob did a very nice article."

"I know that, but you know what I'm talking about."

"Sunny, I'm an adult."

"Yes, you are," Evangelina said, "and we love you.

We don't want to see you getting hurt. Especially considering.'' She gave Griffin an assessing glance.

''Considering?'' he asked.

''You know what I mean.'' Evangelina looked at Abby's abdomen.

''Ah, you think I would take advantage of her situation.''

Abby sputtered. ''You do not have to defend yourself. I didn't bring you here to be grilled.''

''So why did you bring him?'' Joyce Hives asked.

''So you could see that he doesn't have any designs on my person,'' Abby said.

Griffin smiled.

She glared at him.

''Darlin', I told you that I *did* have designs on your person.''

''Well, an honest man at last!'' Sunny said. ''Finally a man who doesn't back away from the truth even when it makes him look bad. Most men would have lied. Except maybe my Chester, or maybe Ellie's Parker. Maybe a few others, but not many. It does look bad to go around saying you want Abby, though, you know,'' she told Griffin.

He slowly shook his head. ''As I told Abby, a man would have to be nerve damaged not to feel desire for her, but wanting and doing are two different things. I have no intention of dishonoring her in any way, I haven't done so in spite of those damning pictures, and I would appreciate it if you would inform any man who does have bad intentions that he'd better back off. Abby is not to be toyed with.'' His voice went rough, his eyes looked suddenly dark and dangerous.

The faces of most of the women in the room took

on a dreamy expression. Some whispering circled the room.

Abby couldn't sit still. She stood up. ''Excuse me, but I am not a mannequin, and I never have been. This is me you're talking about, and I make my own decisions. All of you know that. Except maybe Griffin,'' she said, glaring at him. ''So I'm telling him now. I take care of myself, and I do as I please.''

''So...you're telling me you want the man, and you want us to butt out.'' Sunny crossed her arms and gave that wise-woman look that she managed so well.

''I'm...actually, I—'' Abby hesitated. ''Griffin and I are both grown-ups, and while it's not any of anyone's business but ours, we have no intention of getting involved. He's going back to Chicago soon, and I'm going to get married just as soon as Thomasina finds the right man for me.''

''That's what has me worried,'' Griffin said. ''After that newspaper article appeared, well, any man who saw that and knew that Abby was shopping around—any of Thomasina's customers, that is—might get the wrong idea about what she'll tolerate. So I'd appreciate it if all of you would squelch any rumors if you hear them starting. Abby isn't that kind of woman.''

She blinked and opened her mouth to protest, but what could she say? She wasn't that kind of woman most of the time, the exception to the rule being Griffin? And telling a man she wasn't that kind of woman when the pictures indicated that she was...well, she hadn't even thought of how that article was going to affect her husband hunt.

Still, she didn't like to be coddled. She stood up again. She looked down at Griffin. ''I am perfectly capable of handling the situation,'' she said. ''This is my battle to fight.''

He gazed up at her, his expression unchanging. ''It became mine when I looked at you that way and someone recorded it on film. If not for my slip, you wouldn't be facing this problem.''

''I don't think I have a problem,'' she lied.

Just at that moment Thomasina came through the door. ''Good, I heard the two of you were over here. I've spent the morning fielding offers from men, Abby. I just wanted to let you know, though, that I've screened the calls carefully. Most of them I turned away. Some of them…well…'' She fanned herself with her hand. ''They were most improper, and I sent them packing. None of my female clients need to be subjected to that kind of thing. Still, I think one or two of them might actually do. They were more interested in your horticultural background and the fact that you looked like you enjoyed your work.

''Surprisingly enough, this turned out to be good publicity after I weeded out the wild ones. I've brought along the information on two of the more promising prospects. You just look these profiles over, and see what you think. If anything clicks, I'll set something up.'' And she smiled beatifically. ''I do believe this is going to work, Abby. At least one of these men is very desirable. You're going to be a lovely bride, my dear.''

''Abby, look, look,'' Casey called at that moment, running from the kitchen. ''Ms. Lydia and me, we cut up a cookie and she got some frosting and we made a fish. Just like Bertha,'' he said, naming one of the fish he had chosen yesterday. He flew to her, placed one hand on her knee and held up a cookie, his eyes irresistibly excited.

"Dad, see?" he asked.

Griffin directed a pointed look at Abby's knee, which had smudges of frosting on it. She grinned and shrugged and studied the cookie. "I do believe it is just like Bertha," she said.

And Griffin laughed. "That's one pretty neat cookie, my little baker man. Thank you, son," he said, as Casey broke off two pieces of cookie and gave one to him and one to Abby.

"See, everything's perfect," Abby said. "Thank you, Casey. And thank you, too, Tommy." She took the envelope Thomasina handed her and placed it on the table.

When she looked up, she noticed that Griffin was staring at the envelope, a frown on his face. She knew that he was thinking what she had often thought, that Tommy was too innocent to be careful, but then Tommy wasn't the one going on the date. Abby was, and Abby had learned to be especially careful.

After all, wasn't she wishing that Griffin would take her in his arms and kiss her right now? And wasn't she resisting the urge to launch herself at him and press her lips to his? Didn't she want to feel that heat again and yet again? She wanted to feel his fingers threading through her curls and know the hardness of his body against hers.

She wanted a full night of him in her bed.

But she knew better than to let him know the extent of her desire. She was just going to keep that particular fantasy locked away forever. Whenever the urge to know what it would be like to have Griffin make love to her grew too strong, she would squeeze her eyes shut and count as high as she needed to count. She would talk to her plants, she would dig in the dirt with a ferocity that would drive the desire away.

The truth was that she wasn't at all afraid of what that folder held in store for her. The real danger was standing here, broad-shouldered and handsome, his legs braced, his eyes fierce. Her need to touch Griffin was so great she couldn't remember ever feeling anything this strong. No question, Griffin O'Dell was the true danger to her sanity. He didn't want a wife, and unlike Dennis, he had told her point-blank that he *couldn't* have a wife or another child. This time she knew just where she stood. The facts were indisputable. Griffin would never be more than a very sexy employer, and she'd better realize that and act accordingly.

So yes, she would do just fine with any of these men in the folder. Why not? There was really nothing wrong with them, she was sure. The matchmaker had checked them out, and they had passed muster. The sooner she got involved with one and married him the better. No point in wasting any more time.

Chapter Nine

All right, she was just going to stay here in the greenhouse today, Abby decided four days later. She was not going to Griffin's house. There was enough work here getting the last batch of plantings ready, and besides, if she showed up at the estate, he was going to take one look at her face and know the truth.

Last night she'd been forced to arm wrestle her date. Lucius Alloway had started out talking about his truck and the campground that he owned, but soon he'd gotten around to how lonely life could be stuck in a campground all the time.

She hadn't panicked then. It was only when he started talking about how much he missed the warmth of a woman's body that she'd started edging away.

For a second, she'd thought she saw the bearded man in the distance. Then Lucius had closed in, trapped her and kissed her roughly. She felt nauseous; she heard the sounds of running footsteps behind her. Then she brought her knee up hard.

Lucius had let go, and she'd socked him in the eye. Her hand was still stinging, but she hadn't waited to see what the man she'd hit had looked like after her attack. She'd just bolted and run for her truck.

Now here she was, a miserable mess. She didn't want to call Tommy and tell her what had happened because her friend would be heartsick and frantic and filled with remorse.

She didn't want to let Griffin know, because he would probably go off looking for Lucius, and she didn't want that. The truth was that she prided herself so much on being self-sufficient that she didn't want anyone to know she had nearly let herself get caught in a situation she couldn't handle.

It was humiliating enough admitting it to herself. She certainly didn't want to admit it to anyone else.

And worst of all, Abby hated to acknowledge, but she was still shaking and feeling a little scared. Lucius hadn't done anything but kiss her. She supposed he almost had the right to assume a kiss was okay, given the fact that this date had been one both of them had sought out for the purpose of finding a mate. No doubt a kiss was all he had been looking for. But for a moment his arms had felt like ropes of steel, trapping her, caging her, and she realized that for all her brave talk, she wasn't as strong as she wanted everyone to believe. Actually, she was pretty weak in some respects.

And if she was in Griffin's presence for even a minute, she wasn't at all sure that she wouldn't do something really, really stupid. Like ask him to hold her.

''Aagh! Just stop that, will you?'' she yelled, shaking the begonia she was getting ready to pot.

''That's it. You tell him, Abby.'' Griffin's low voice dipped into her consciousness, and she whirled, still holding the innocent plant. Griffin, all lean denim-clad legs and muscle, was leaning against the door to the greenhouse, a good thirty feet away. He seemed disinclined to come any farther into the room.

Under other circumstances, she would have blushed to have been caught, looking like she was disciplining a flower. Today, though, she was just grateful that he didn't know exactly what she had been yelling about.

She lifted one shoulder. "Okay, you caught me again. I was bad-mouthing a begonia. It's my right as a horticulturist."

He nodded slowly but he didn't smile. "You're probably right. I won't criticize."

She waited, unsure what to say.

"I was worried when you didn't show up," he said. His gaze never left her face. She felt rooted in this space, unable to move away from him or move toward him, either. He had that big an effect on her.

"I—" She shook her head, sending her hair sliding against her cheeks. "I thought I'd catch up on a few things I've neglected around here. I would have shown up eventually. There's not that much more left to do, anyway. At least not until the tennis courts are completely finished and I can plant around them."

"And then that will be the last," he said.

"Yes." Her voice felt small. She felt even smaller, as if she were slipping away. Did it have anything to do with the fact that she didn't want to think about the days when she wouldn't have an excuse to see Griffin anymore? For a second she closed her eyes.

"Are you all right, Abby?" he asked, and when she opened her eyes, he had moved much closer. Too close for her to trust herself to act sensibly and yet not nearly close enough for her to touch. Oh damn.

"Abby?"

She managed to nod and lift her chin. She even managed a trace of a smile. "Actually, I'm fine. I guess I should tell you that the date didn't go well last night, but…you know, I was proud of myself. When things weren't going well, I left."

And she was surprised to realize how true that was. She *was* proud of herself. She had considered the fact that Lucius might feel that he had a right to a kiss, but she had felt uncomfortable and she had claimed her right to say no. She had exited before things had gotten completely out of control.

"He touched you."

"Not much."

Griffin's eyes narrowed. "Anything you don't want is too much."

"I know that. I handled it."

"What did you do?"

"I kneed him in the groin, hit him in the eye and then I ran like crazy." She pushed her chin even higher. Her voice was defiant.

She surprised a weary smile from Griffin. "You are something else. You know that?"

"Are you laughing at me?" She squeezed the begonia tight, as tears began to fill her throat. "What would you have suggested I do?"

Griffin silently moved closer, right into her personal space, and the poor mangled plant slipped from her fingers. "Nothing. You did what was needed. You were strong, you were brave."

She managed a small laugh at that. "No, I wasn't. You weren't there."

And that elicited a growl from him. "If he touches you again, if any man touches you and you don't want him to, you do just what you did last night. If that doesn't work you do this." And he showed her how to reach out in what looked like a friendly move and yet could still bend a person backward by pressing their thumb back. "Or you use your legs." And he slid his foot behind hers and shifted suddenly, throwing her off balance. He caught her before she fell. She was in his arms now, bent back over his arm like a dancer, but she wasn't afraid. Not at all. His lips were separated from hers by only a few centimeters of inconsequential air, but she didn't want to move away.

"Take a self-defense course when you get a chance," he said. "Do that for yourself and the baby. And also for the peace of mind of the people who care about you."

"I will," she promised on a breath. "Don't tell Tommy."

His gaze got fiercer. "She has to know."

"It will hurt her."

"It will hurt her more if she sends that guy out with another woman and something even worse happens."

She stared at him, pain and horror filling her.

"You're right. I hadn't thought of that. I'll tell her."

He started to ease her up. "Griffin?"

"Yes." He slid his hands more firmly behind her back, but stopped his movement otherwise.

She bit her lip, unsure what exactly she wanted to say. She only knew that she wanted something. People knew her here. They worried, but they couldn't make her feel safe. Griffin made her feel safe. "Thank you. For the tips. And for caring what happens to me and the baby. You're a good man."

He closed his eyes. "You are so wrong," he said when he opened them. And then he leaned forward and kissed her. Gently. Fully. He covered her lips. He brushed her mouth with his, once, twice before he started to move away.

Reason crumbled. She snaked her arms around his neck tightly and kissed him back, loosening all the passion she'd been hiding and holding inside herself.

He pulled back just a breath, his expression worried, asking her something.

''Don't,'' was all she could get out, and she hoped he would know that she meant ''Don't go, don't stop kissing me.'' She hoped that her eyes told him what her words hadn't.

And then he lifted her. He lowered his mouth to hers as he gathered her into his arms. The greenhouse disappeared. The world vanished in a hazy mist. All that mattered was Griffin, his warm masculine scent, the way his fingers splayed against her spine, the way his big body fit to hers and the thrill of feeling his lips brushing hers. Abby threaded her fingers through Griffin's dark hair. She tasted him and pressed closer.

He tilted his head to deepen the kiss, sending heat whirling through her. He stood legs apart with Abby snug against his hips. It was as close as they could get and still remain clothed. He raked his hands up her sides, his thumbs resting just beneath the swell of her breasts, and Abby nearly lost her mind.

Somewhere in the distance she heard a bell. A telephone. The sound was soft, but it was as if a gong had gone off near their heads.

Griffin released her, only waiting to make sure she was steady before letting her go.

''Hell, Abby. Slap me or something,'' he said, and he didn't look one bit happy.

''You know I'm not going to do that.''

"Well, you should. Heck, if I could slap myself, I would. And you didn't do any of the things I told you to do if a man should try to take advantage," he whispered roughly.

She didn't answer. He knew darn well that she had wanted him to take advantage. She had been the one who had forged ahead with the kiss at first, but he had a point. She had no business wanting anything from him or he from her. Their paths shouldn't be crossing this way. She didn't know what to say, but she knew that she couldn't leave things this way. Everything felt too raw and serious. She couldn't let him think that anything but pure lust had been involved here, even though she had a horrible suspicion that what she had been feeling had gone well beyond desire.

He didn't want that. For sure, *she* didn't want it.

"Abby, say something," he coaxed. "Say something brutal to me if you won't hit me."

"Well, I *was* going to hit you," she said, trying for levity. "I was just waiting until you were really involved. Then I was going to let you have it," she lied.

He shook his head and attempted a small laugh. "I'll be more careful around you in future," he said, his voice still thick and smoky. "That's a promise…a good one."

They stood there in silence.

Finally Griffin cleared his throat. "Abby, I know why you didn't come by this morning. It was because of last night, wasn't it?"

She shrugged. "I might have needed some time to collect my thoughts after the thing with Lucius."

"You didn't feel safe last night. I want you to feel safe at my home," he told her.

"I do."

He looked skeptical. "After today?" he asked.

"I do," she said again, touching his arm. "Don't worry about that kiss," she said. "It didn't mean a thing. I mean, we've both admitted that we have this unnerving desire that we're doing our best to ignore. And maybe sometimes we're not doing a real good job of ignoring it, but we're trying. So, don't think I was hiding because I was afraid to be around you. That wasn't it at all. I just figured that if you knew about Lucius, you might do something rash. Like bust some heads or something."

He raised one dark brow. "Sounds like a plan."

"I don't want that," she said. "I told you before, I want to do things myself."

"You are. I wasn't there last night. I didn't help you."

She tilted her head. "Maybe you did. You're so suspicious of my matchmaking plan, so suspicious of every man that Tommy sends me that I was on the alert for something. I was already in the ready-to-make-an-escape mode when he grabbed me. After that, it was only a matter of getting loose. And since I was already ready to go, and you'd made such a point of me watching out for myself, I didn't question my right to strike back the way I might have in the past. Now that I think about it, if Lucius Alloway has a black eye, it's probably mainly your fault. If he sues me, I'll send him your way."

Griffin gave her a long, slow grin. "You send him my way anytime you want, darlin'. Good old Lucius and I will talk."

She smiled back at him. "The point I'm trying to make, Griffin, is that I'm not nervous being around you."

"No?" He gave her speculative look.

Well yes, she was nervous, but not in a bad way.

"Does that mean you'll come back to work?"

The pressure of his kiss was still on her lips. Her body was still throbbing. She wasn't sure she could trust herself not to wrap her body around his again today.

"Come with me," he coaxed. "Casey made another batch of cookies, and he's missing you."

"That's fighting dirty, like a rat," she said, wrinkling her nose.

"A rat is what I am, darlin', and don't you forget it."

She could argue, but he'd only argue back. "I'll come," she finally said on a laugh. "And don't you go touching any of my cookies."

"Your cookies are safe," he promised, but as he turned to go, he brushed her lips lightly with his thumb.

Abby stood staring after him even as his car drove off down the road. "It's not really my cookies I'm worried about, Griff," she whispered. "That's not the part of me that's in danger."

Griffin drove away feeling like a total worm. He had completely lost his head when Abby had been in his arms. Even now desire ran thick through his body, and that just couldn't continue. But even worse was the horrible feeling that he had betrayed Abby's trust. Nick Sevren, the detective he had hired the first time Tommy had set Abby up on a date, had been there watching last night. He'd told Griffin what had happened, and the thought of that and of what might have happened had driven Griffin wild. He'd had to come see Abby and find out if she was all right.

But he hadn't been prepared for the mile-deep guilt

that had hit him, knowing he had set a spy to watch her. She was so brave. She'd been so proud of herself for handling the situation. Her independence was so very important to her. How had he ignored that when she'd made it so clear, and how could he tell her that he'd sent a bodyguard to watch over her? Not once, but twice.

He couldn't. It would damage her pride too much. All he could do was tell Nick that he wouldn't be needing his services anymore.

Was it true? Not really. He was, if anything, even more worried about Abby than he had been before. He didn't want her meeting up with another guy like Lucius, ever, but he just couldn't betray her trust anymore. In doing that, he was worse than the man who attacked her. He became the man who ran the risk of hurting her inside rather than outside.

"Okay, but there's one area where I am still going to interfere, and that's in making sure Tommy knows the whole truth about last night. That's the absolute bottom line, O'Dell," he told himself. He knew Abby would tell her matchmaker friend about the madness of the night before, but he also knew that Abby's soft heart might keep her from making things as clear as they should be. That might mean that Abby would be put in danger again. He couldn't live with that. He definitely couldn't go away and think about something like that happening to her again. So, he was going to have to suggest to Tommy that she invest in some professional help in doing background checks. Maybe he would even suggest Nick as a possible contact.

And, oh, yes, there was one more thing he had to do, or at least say.

"Keep your own paws off Abby from here on out,"

he ordered himself. "You, O'Dell, are the very last man she needs messing up her life. Control yourself." He would do that except…he couldn't control himself when he was dreaming.

Abby had been with him in his bed for the past few nights.

"All right, are you ready to get dirty?" Abby asked five days later. She gazed up at the two males standing beside her. Since this was the last flower bed she would plant, she had promised Casey that he could help. His eager blue eyes told her that he was looking forward to it. Griffin's carefully controlled smile told her that he was not so enthused. She understood. Her own stomach was doing triple flips. For the past few days they had kept their distance, kept things completely professional.

It had been torture.

It had been smart. She had watched from a distance as Griffin had walked the grounds, dodging the scores of workers scrambling to finish their tasks before the first clients arrived. Griff had held his son's hand tightly, gazing at him with such fierce love that it made her heart ache for him, to know he could only have this short part of the year. He had given Casey piggy back rides, taken him with him everywhere, played catch and tag and hide-and-seek. Mrs. Digner had told Abby that Griffin ate anything that Casey cooked, even the inedible stuff. And now here he was, getting ready to plant flowers with a woman he really wanted to stay away from, just because his child wanted it so badly.

This was going to be exquisitely painful. Thank goodness she had had such a tough background. She knew how to handle pain and how to hide her true expression.

''Tell us what you want us to do, Abby,'' Griffin urged in those low, strong tones. And she longed to tell him exactly what she wanted him to do. She wanted him to be the kind of man Tommy would match her up with, a man who wanted to start a new family, a man who would stay and who would love her.

She shied away from the word, closed her heart to her thoughts. Love wasn't what she had asked Tommy for, and it certainly wasn't what she really wanted or needed.

''This is going to be great,'' she said, doing her best to get into the spirit of things. ''We've planted the shrubs around the tennis courts. Now we're just going to add a little color. Some blue, some gold and just a touch of lavender.''

''Lavender?'' Casey asked, looking confused.

''Purple,'' Griffin said, and Abby blushed. There was so much she didn't know about children. ''But lavender is a great new word, don't you think?''

''Lavender,'' Casey said. ''Lavender, lavender, lavender. I like lavender. Hey, Abby.''

''Hey, Casey,'' she countered with a smile.

''You have lavender,'' he said, patting a patch on her patchwork blouse. ''Now you, Dad.'' He showed Griffin where to pat.

''It's definitely lavender,'' Griffin agreed. ''But we don't touch, son, unless we're asked to.''

Casey's eyes looked troubled, guilty.

''It's all right,'' Abby said soothingly. ''You can touch, Casey. Let's get this plant in the ground. It needs a home and water,'' she added, hastily whisking past the touching topic, all too aware that Casey would want her to ask Griffin to touch, too.

So for the next half hour the three of them made magic with flowers.

"That was nicely done," Griffin whispered near her ear when Casey had wandered off to chase after an errant chipmunk.

Abby felt Griffin's warm breath at her ear. She turned to find him kneeling just behind her.

"I'm learning," she said with a small smile. "Casey is a good teacher. He makes the thought of being a mother less frightening."

"You're going to be a great mother," he said, leaning closer.

"I don't know." She looked down at her spade, concentrating furiously on the ground before her.

And then he moved until he was beside her. He gently touched her chin, turning her to face him. "I know," he said. "He adores you. You're wonderful with him."

"So are you."

"It's not the same. I'm his father. I love him. You were good with him from the start." Which saved her from telling the truth, that she loved his little boy, too.

"Well, this is so very, very interesting. Quite." A woman's husky voice cut into Abby's thoughts, just as she heard Griffin swear beneath his breath.

A tall, slender blond woman wearing a pale-blue knee-length suit that probably cost more than all of Red Rose was worth stood, arms crossed, staring at Abby and Griffin. Her pale-blue pumps were sinking into the new sod, and yet she still looked dignified and beautiful. And extremely angry.

"Mama! Mama!" Casey came running toward the woman full tilt.

She held out her arms. "How are you, my baby?

Heavens, but you're dirty!'' She cast an accusing glance at Griffin.

Abby suddenly felt like a combination of prostitute and the awkward tomboy she'd once been. She carefully sat back on her heels and began gathering her gardening equipment.

''He's fine, Cheryl,'' Griffin said, rising to his feet. ''Abby's been teaching him about flowers.''

''I'm sure,'' Cheryl said, making it obvious that she was sure her son had been exposed to all kinds of improper scenarios between his father and the gardener. ''I saw the pictures from the paper. Someone mailed them to me.''

Abby ventured a glance up. Griffin was looking grim. ''Then you probably also saw the publication they were printed in, and you knew not to jump to the wrong conclusions.''

Except, Abby thought, were they the wrong conclusions? Hadn't she lusted after this man? Hadn't he admitted that he wanted her? And wasn't it clearly a case of overactive hormones, since there couldn't be anything serious going on?

''I know what I saw, Griffin. And what Casey must have seen.''

Griffin's jaw looked like a knife blade. He blew out a breath that made Abby look up. When she did, she saw that he was holding out his hand to her. ''We're being rude, Cheryl, in case you hadn't noticed. I'd like you to meet Abigail Chesney. She's an artist with plants.''

Abby stared at his hand. She was filthy, dirtier even than he was, and his ex-wife, the woman he still might have feelings for, the mother of his child, was watching. Did he really expect her to take his hand?

He waited. Clearly he did.

She glanced at Cheryl, who was looking even more imperious and dignified and exotically lovely. The woman was staring at Abby as if she were naked in public, or possibly sporting a pair of horns and a forked tail. Abby felt exposed, the same way she had once in first grade when a well-meaning teacher had insisted that she make a Father's Day present like the other kids, even though she had no father. And just as it had then, anger reared up in her.

She carefully placed her hand in Griffin's and rose to her feet as regally as she could, given the fact that she had been kneeling for some time. When she stood, her shirt pressed against her belly, and Cheryl's gaze settled there.

"How nice for you," she said.

"Yes," Abby said simply. "Good morning, Ms.—"

"Mrs. Finnson," Griffin supplied.

"Good morning, Mrs. Finnson," Abby said.

"Ah, but it's afternoon, Abby. It is Abby, isn't it? I forget. Griffin meets so many women. Time flies when you're with him, doesn't it? At least when he's around. He hardly ever is, you know."

"Cheryl." Griffin looked pointedly at Casey, and for just a moment Abby thought that the woman actually looked a bit guilty.

"Come, baby," she told her son. "Stuart's here. Do you want to see him?"

"I like Stuart," Casey said to Abby. "Can we show him our…our zin things?"

Abby hesitated. "If he wishes. You did do a wonderful job on the zinnias, Casey." Angry mother or no angry mother, she was not going to let anyone make Casey feel less than proud of what he'd done today.

"Okay. Dad, Mom, Abby," Casey said. "Let's see Stuart."

And so, like unhappy puppets the three of them walked to the car. Stuart, a tall, dour-looking blond man, dutifully came to the garden and gave Casey a pat on the back. "Looks like you learned something today," he said.

"Abby showed me. Abby talks to fwowers." He said it with pride, as if Abby communed with wizards and goblins.

And Griffin grinned.

Cheryl glared.

"We'll discuss things later, Griffin," she said. "I didn't come here to talk about gardening."

"I'm hoping you came to see just how right this place is for Casey and me," he said, not budging.

But his ex-wife didn't answer, and Abby knew as well as Griffin did why Cheryl Finnson had come to Red Rose. She wanted ammunition to use against Griffin, and *Lindsey Junction NewsNotes* had supplied her with just what she needed.

Unless something happened, the woman was going to make some serious trouble for Griffin and his child.

Abby's heart broke at the thought. She wondered if there was anything Griffin could do. He was a powerful man. He'd told her that he already had clients waiting in line to come visit the O'Dell mansion once the work was completed. Now that she knew him, she'd started paying more attention to the business pages. His company and his contributions to the company were mentioned often.

One night when she couldn't sleep, she'd looked him up on the Internet. It was all there to read, his rough beginnings, his success at an early age, the companies he'd made and bought and sold, the women he'd dated, the one he'd married and the failure of that marriage. The one constant was Griffin's ability to turn a failing company into one that made other businessmen envious. He could do almost anything in most people's eyes.

But not in his. He'd told her he wasn't good at relationships, his marriage had ended unhappily, and he was uninterested in beginning another. He could do almost anything except love a woman forever.

What could he do when a woman who had once lived with him decided to take away the one thing he loved beyond life itself—his child?

And was there anything that Abby could do to right this situation?

Chapter Ten

Well, Thomasina Edgerton just might not be as much of a pushover as he'd pegged her to be, Griffin conceded when he was midway through his conversation with her the next day.

"As I mentioned the other day, Abby told me what happened with Lucius," the woman said. "I assure you that I've had a chance to talk to him since then, and I gave him a serious tongue lashing. He will not be a client of mine anymore. Furthermore, I had already considered what you have suggested, a private detective. I'm not well versed in such things, but I'll certainly educate myself before I hire someone. And I will."

It occurred to Griffin then that Tommy might not have the money to pay an employee. He'd brought this subject up several days ago, and he hadn't even thought of her finances. Matchmaking couldn't be lucrative work, especially if the results were as disappointing as Abby's had been so far.

"A detective will probably expect to work on an hourly or daily rate."

"I'll find one who will work on a profit-sharing basis, on a commission if you will."

Griffin blinked. "I doubt that will work."

Thomasina took a deep breath and stood taller. "I'll make it work."

And she would be disappointed. There would be no one checking out the men who wanted to date Abby.

"Perhaps I can help in some way."

She stared at him. "You will not pay anyone. I'll do it."

Okay, chalk one up for the matchmaker. He didn't bother denying that was the first thought that had entered his mind. "I might know someone who would be willing to do things your way. He's good, and I promise I won't pay him."

She hesitated, then she nodded curtly. "I would appreciate it, then."

"Don't let her get hurt, Tommy."

"I won't. I promise."

"Don't settle for less than she deserves."

Tommy raised a brow and looked at him sternly. She crossed her arms. "I know just what she wants, Griffin. She wants a good, simple, ordinary man, a quiet man who will settle down and stay. A man who will be a friend and not much more."

Griffin nodded tightly. He knew what Tommy was telling him. He had better keep his distance, because he wasn't what Abby wanted.

Some other lucky man would be the one she chose.

"That woman came to the Red Rose today," Sunny told Abby later that day. "She was asking a lot of nosy questions."

''What did you tell her?''

''She told her to stop being so nosy,'' Lydia said with a laugh. ''But seriously, Abby, watch out. That woman means to cause trouble for you or for Griffin.''

''I'm afraid she was asking me questions, too,'' Tommy said. The matchmaker had dropped in for a rare visit to the diner. ''She must have heard that you were using my services. I didn't tell her anything, of course.'' But then Tommy grew still and pink. ''She might also have heard that her ex-husband had been by to see me once or twice.''

''Griffin?'' Abby's voice came out a big high. ''Is he…looking?''

''He's worried about you and the Lucius thing,'' Tommy said. ''He's convinced me to try this Mr. Sevren, his detective friend. To do background checks. And don't look at me that way, Abigail Chesney. I'm beginning to think that Griffin O'Dell has hidden qualities. It's to his credit that he's concerned about you.''

''Yes, it is.'' But that was just the kind of man he was. There were plenty of well-documented cases of Griffin watching out for his employees. She'd read of his kindnesses when she had looked him up on the Net.

Later, as they walked out of the diner together, Tommy turned to her. ''What happened after Griffin found out about Lucius? He seemed pretty upset.''

Abby felt the heat rising through her body. She knew Griffin had been upset about what had happened on her date, but he was probably even more upset about that heated embrace she had shared with him.

''Nothing much happened.''

''Define 'nothing much.'''

''Exactly that. Nothing much. We talked. He showed me some ways to protect myself.''

''Ways that involved touching?''

''Of course ways that involved touching, Tommy.'' Abby couldn't help it. Her voice was defensive. She was sure her face was hot pink. She did what she seldom did and looked away.

Tommy sighed. Abby knew that sigh. It signaled frustration. ''A man like that is a rarity,'' Tommy said.

''Don't even go where you're going.''

''At least admit that you're attracted.''

''Every woman is attracted.''

''Every woman isn't you, and it's you I'm talking about. He didn't come around asking me to watch out for Delia or Sunny or Joyce. It's you he's worried about.''

''That's because I'm the only one going out with men I've never met.''

''Not true.''

Abby turned, a question in her eyes.

''No, it's confidential,'' Tommy said. ''Look, just admit that what you feel for Griffin is out of the ordinary.''

They had reached Abby's car. She shook her head as she opened the door. ''Don't go there, Tommy. You're headed down a dead-end street.'' Because, attracted though she might be, she couldn't allow herself to even venture near what Tommy was thinking. If she did, she was going to get hurt big-time, bigger than she'd ever been hurt before. Griffin had made no secret of his temporary nature and soon enough he would be going, going, gone.

She had better put some extra padding around her heart and get her mind back on safer paths.

As for tonight, she needed distraction, something to do.

''What did Griffin's ex-wife ask you?'' she asked as she prepared to drive away.

''She asked me if you were living with Griffin,'' Tommy said.

''And you told her…''

''That I didn't gossip about my friends. She said that she didn't need my information. She would find out on her own. She also said that she intended to find out a great many things, and she meant to do some things, too. Griffin had better watch his back.''

But it wasn't his back he was worried about, Abby knew. It was his son.

Her time with Griffin was over in any real sense. Her presence had already created a real problem for him. Abby had no doubt that Cheryl Finnson was going to do her best to paint Griffin in a bad light, and to take Casey from him. All she needed to do was find one person who was willing to say a few negative things about Abby and Griffin, to imply that they had knowledge that Griffin had been having sex with his employee while his child was at home, and the woman might make a case for keeping Casey in her possession for even longer than she already had him.

And who would have any wish to harm either Griffin or Abby?

Someone who had had a run-in with one of them lately.

Like Lucius Alloway? Could Cheryl do that? Would she ever find anything out about that incident? Would she actually stoop so low as to use it? Would Lucius lie and say that Abby had been the one at fault?

There was no way of knowing, but Cheryl was angry,

and she was asking plenty of questions. Sooner or later someone would slip and give the wrong answer.

And Griffin's ex-wife might try to take Casey. Maybe she'd fail, and maybe she wouldn't, but either way Griffin and possibly Casey would end up getting hurt.

Unless someone did something.

Closing her mind to what she was about to do, Abby drove to the Red Rose Heaven Hotel. She asked Barbara Marie at the desk to direct her to Cheryl's room, and then she took a deep breath, went down the hall and knocked on the door. She held her hands against the legs of her jeans because they were already beginning to perspire. She half hoped that Cheryl would still be out.

But that hope died when Cheryl opened the door. She was wearing pencil-slim black pants and a white blouse. The outfit should have looked plain, but with model-perfect looks like Cheryl's, plain wasn't a possibility.

"Well, look who's here," Cheryl said. She gestured Abby inside.

"I suppose you're wondering what I want," Abby said.

"I'm assuming you're going to tell me."

Abby stared at Cheryl, who wore a knowing smile. "You've been asking lots of questions about me. Perhaps you'd like to ask them in person."

Cheryl shook her head. "That isn't necessary. I know everything I want to know."

Which could mean anything. It could mean she'd gotten hold of Lucius. It could mean she was bluffing.

"Look," Abby said. "It's obvious we've gotten off to a bad start, but I just wanted to tell you that Griffin has been a good father while I've been there. It's clear he loves Casey, that he would give his life for his son.

I don't think there is anything that would convince him to do anything that might harm your son in any way, Mrs. Finnson."

"Oh, come now, call me Cheryl, since we're being so cozy. And please, Abby, since you're being so frank, let me be equally frank. Your heart is showing, honey."

Abby blinked.

"Oh, don't look so surprised. It's written on every inch of your face. Anyone with clear vision can see it. Not a surprise, Abby. Griffin is, after all, a superbly good-looking man, dressed or undressed. I understand the appeal. I fell for those looks once, and I'm sure no one faults you for falling for them, too. But don't come here begging for mercy for him. It's just not going to happen. Now, if you'll excuse me..." She nodded toward the door.

"I'm not in love with Griffin," Abby said, suddenly, awkwardly. "That's not why I came."

Cheryl chuckled. "Of course it isn't, Miss Chesney. And you know, I'd love to discuss this further, but I just can't. Stuart is out, but he'll be back soon. We have things to do."

And Abby didn't know what to say. If she continued to protest, that would just give Cheryl more reason to believe that she was in love with Griffin. It certainly would do nothing to help his case. Reluctantly she left the room and the hotel. When she arrived back home, she sank down onto her porch, her elbows propped on her knees. She had just been bested in an argument, she hadn't even put up a fight, she who had learned how to argue at her mother's knee. It was frustrating. It was irritating, and she had barely even let out a whimper. Cheryl's accusations about Abby being in love with

Griffin had caught her off guard, especially when she had said that everyone could tell.

Abby felt her hands growing cold and clammy.

Cheryl was probably calling Griffin right now to laugh about the fact that Abby had come to plead for him.

What would he think? Especially when she, a woman who had just given him the big talk about hating it when people interfered in her life, 'fessed up?

''I don't know, but you have to tell him,'' she whispered. ''You broke your own rule, and now everything is worse for him. Now she thinks she has more ammo, and thinking you have something is half the battle. You've hurt him with your nosing in, Abby. Do something.''

She would, just as soon as she'd had a night to think and think straight this time, she would do something. Hopefully something helpful.

Abby hadn't been at work for two days, Griffin thought, tossing up a baseball and drilling it into the batting cage with a one-thousand-dollar baseball bat he'd planned on christening with his visiting clients. Too bad. He needed distraction. He needed to hit something hard. No, what he really needed was to see Abby, but he hadn't been able to bring himself to ask her why she was avoiding him.

He knew why. Cheryl had been planting the seeds of something ugly. He didn't want to make it worse for Abby by playing into his ex-wife's hands. The happiness of two people, Abby and Casey, was at stake here. He didn't want to risk making a wrong step that might harm them. And there was a third person's happiness at stake, as well. His own. If anything happened with Casey or Abby, he wasn't going to be able to forgive himself. If he thought humbling himself before Cheryl would work, he'd do it. But it had never worked before. So he waited things out.

And he missed Abby.

So when he looked up four hours later and saw her blue truck pulling into the drive, it was all he could do not to rush out and grab her into his arms.

He forced himself to be still and wait. He knew the routines by now. She would busy herself with her plants and her dirt and not come near the house. She would pretend that he had never kissed her, and that she had never returned that kiss. As if he could ever forget the feel of soft cotton covering her warm skin as he pressed her to him, as if he could set aside the throbbing of his body whenever she got more than a few feet from him.

But she needed to pretend that there was nothing but business between them, and maybe he needed her to be that way, too. It made it easier to imagine the day when he and Casey would pack up and leave for the rest of the year.

So he would wait. He'd give her maybe five or ten minutes before he went down there and asked if she was all right.

Because he knew darn well that she wasn't all right. Strong and brave as she was, Cheryl's insinuations had hurt her. How could they not? She had already been worrying that she wouldn't be a good mom. Now she was probably worrying that she might have hurt Casey. As if she could do that.

He waited.

But the truck didn't stop out in the area where Abby had left off planting the other day. It headed on and kept coming, all the way up to the house.

And that meant one thing. Something was wrong.

Griffin strode to the door and stared down at Abby just as she made it to the porch.

She looked up at him with anguished eyes.

"Don't do that," he said.

"What?"

"I don't know, but whatever you're blaming yourself for, don't do it."

"You don't know what I did."

"You'll tell me, and it will be fine. Come inside." And then he touched her. He took her hand, felt it warm and soft and fragile beneath his fingers.

But he had forgotten her need to be strong. She pulled back on her hand. "No," she said. "I want to talk to you, but I don't want to upset Casey. Is he inside?"

Griffin gave a quick nod. "Yes, but he's upstairs napping. Hard morning playing. We have some time. Come in." And this time she let him touch her and draw her into the house.

They had always gone to the kitchen, the heart of the house done in oak and white and blue and filled with light. But it was open, and Mrs. Digner might come in at any minute. Instead, Griffin led Abby to the library, decorated in blue and dark gold. Books lined the mahogany shelves, and there were deep cushy chairs made for reading or resting. As if any of that mattered today.

"Have a seat," he suggested, motioning toward an alcove where two chairs sat half-turned toward each other. "We can talk here."

"I can stand. I won't be here that long."

"That sounds ominous."

"Not ominous, just honest. I want you to know that I…I went to see your ex-wife. At her hotel room, I mean."

Griffin blinked. Abby was standing there defiantly, her chin thrust upward, her feet spread in a fighter's stance, but while that part of her body language suggested bravery, he couldn't help noticing that she had made a cradle of her arms around her baby. She was swaying from one foot to the other.

He ducked his head in acknowledgment. "No rule against that. She said some things to you. Maybe you had some things to say to her."

Abby blew out a breath. "I absolutely don't believe that you are for real. These are fighting words, Griffin. Listen to what I'm saying. I'm telling you that I went to confront your ex-wife, a move that was completely out of line given the fact that I am merely your… your—"

"Watch it," he warned.

"Your gardener," she said, enunciating the syllables. "I had no business getting involved in your personal affairs."

The look in her eyes, the way her voice dropped to a choked whisper, nearly made Griffin's heart stop. What had gone on in that hotel room? What had Cheryl said to her?

"What happened?" he asked, and the words came out too forcefully, almost like an accusation.

She twisted her hands together, then drew herself up and held her arms to her sides, standing as tall and proud as he'd ever seen her. "I went to see Cheryl to explain to her what a good father you were. I was afraid that she might try to hurt you and Casey because of those pictures. I thought I might be able to convince her that what she'd seen had been a lie."

"But it wasn't a lie."

"It was," she declared hotly. "We agreed that even

if we were attracted, it didn't mean anything. I don't want it to mean anything.''

Somehow Griffin managed to let that comment slide by, past the pain that settled deep inside him. ''So...what did Cheryl say to you?''

Abby shook her head.

''Did she tell you just how wrong you were, that I had been a hell of a bad husband and father?''

''No, she...''

''She should have. I was, Abby. I lived for work, I left them alone. I barely saw Casey his first two years. Anything she said I deserved.''

''But you adore him. Anyone can see that.''

''Yes, because I almost lost him, and then, only then, did I realize how much precious time I had lost. She hates me, but I don't blame her for it. I only blame her for not wanting to let me go on being the right kind of father this time.''

''That's why I went. Those pictures give her ammunition, don't they?''

He didn't want to admit it, but she was right. ''That isn't your fault. Not any of it.''

''Oh yes, it is.'' She looked up at him then, fiercely. She firmed her lips. ''I made it worse. By going there, I made it much worse.'' Her cheeks turned deliciously pink.

And Griffin saw. ''She thought you were pleading for mercy for your lover.''

Abby didn't shrink from his gaze. ''Yes.'' And then she visibly swallowed. He wanted to reach out and comfort her, but given Cheryl's accusations, that could only hurt her more. She looked as if she might shatter, this brave, wonderful woman. He'd done that to her, him and his situation.

"I should never have interfered," Abby said, rushing on. "Aren't I always the one who tells everyone just how much I abhor people interfering in my life? I preach that every day, and yet I just ignored my own rules. I had to tell you."

"What? That you'd interfered on my behalf?"

"Yes, and things are so much worse now," she said. "Here." She reached back into her jeans and pulled out a slip of paper.

Griffin frowned. He knew darn well what she was giving him. That couldn't be anything but the contract the two of them had drawn up. She started to tear it in two.

"No." He reached out and touched her hand.

Her fingers trembled. She pulled back, but she didn't rip up the contract. "My job here is almost finished, anyway," she argued. "Almost anyone can do the rest of the work."

"Dammit, Abby, you think I'd want to fire you because you tried to help me?"

"Are you arguing with me again, O'Dell?"

He studied her. "If you're trying to leave before we're done, then yes, I guess I am."

"Didn't you hear me? What I did hurt you and Casey. And no, I don't really think you're the kind of man who would dismiss me for trying to help, even if you were angry with me. That's why I'm firing myself."

"I don't care if it didn't turn out the way you wanted it to. Your intentions were good."

"You don't care that now she has ammunition that might take Casey from you?"

That stopped him cold. "I hate the fact that she would even try, but that isn't your fault. She would have tried anyway. If it hadn't been this, it would have been something else. Cheryl hates me with a passion, and she knows just where to hit me. Add to that the fact that hitting me gives her more of Casey, and there just isn't much she wouldn't do to make me out to be even worse than I am. It wasn't your doing.''

Abby didn't speak, but she still looked unconvinced. She swung away from him, and he saw that she was going to leave.

''Abby, you came to me to confess what seemed like a sin to you, but I sinned against you and never confessed.''

''What do you mean?'' She turned around, her eyes wary, her voice strained.

''Meaning I interfered in your life when I know how you feel about such things.''

Her eyes begged him to explain.

''Those two dates you went on, I had you followed.''

''You what?''

He could barely force himself to look her in the eye as he confessed, but she had been brave enough to face him when she told him about going to see Cheryl. How could he do less?

''I was…very worried about your safety. I hired a private detective, a bodyguard, if you will, to make sure that no one hurt you in any way.''

She stepped nearer, quietly moving into his space. Griffin had never felt so much like a bad boy. He'd been an honest businessman, but there were always moments when a businessman, if he was successful, had to make tough decisions. He was good at forging ahead during such moments, but here, confessing to Abby that he had sicced a bodyguard on her, he felt as if he wanted to fall to his knees and beg her forgiveness.

''The bearded man,'' she said suddenly.

"Yes."

"You could have told me."

"You would have told me that you had the situation under control."

"I would have been right."

"I know that now."

"Was he there that second time?"

"Much farther away. I…felt guilty. I didn't want him intruding on your privacy."

She started to turn, then she turned back. "Did he report on everything we said or did?"

"Damn it, no. I did not send him to spy on you or report your activities to me." Hot anger filled him, but none of it was directed at her. He was seeing his actions through her eyes now, and he didn't like what he saw. "Abby, I'm sorry. I should never have interfered in your plans. It won't happen again."

"Even if I tell you I'm going out with a man with eight hands and a lecherous desire to bed the next woman he sees?"

Griffin swallowed hard. He counted to ten, and then to twenty. He did it twice.

"Griffin?"

"You're on your own in the dating scene, Abby. Hands off from here on out." And he held out his empty hands to show her that he meant what he said.

"This doesn't change things, you know," she whispered. "Just because you interfered doesn't change the harm I caused."

"Then how about this? I don't want you to go."

She bit her lip. "That can't count. We're just an employer and employee."

"You know we're more than that."

She closed her eyes. "I don't want you to be more."

"I know. Neither do I, but…we're friends. At the very least we've become friends. Haven't we?"

He couldn't help it then. He touched her. He took one cold hand in his own and ran his thumb over her palm. She shivered and opened her eyes. Her lips were trembling. She hesitated, and he thought he might go crazy waiting for her response. Because he would abide by it. He cared about her too much to ignore her wishes.

"Friends," she finally agreed. "But not for long. A few weeks and you'll be gone. Besides, I'm almost done here."

"Maybe not. I'm having my first guests here next week. And even though I've converted the old barn into a warehouse and have stocked it with my newest products and had most of the sports fields completed, there are things that aren't quite finished here. I'm probably rushing things, but I wanted to let a few of my better clients in on the planning stages. They'll want to know all the details of how everything was accomplished. They'll want to see the before and after pictures, and they'll want to meet the woman who added the fountains and the flowers and the ponds and turned a few ordinary green fields into a magical fairyland."

"You could tell them." She sounded just too darn hopeful. He squeezed her hand.

Somehow he managed to laugh. "I could tell them I have red and blue flowers. That's not what they're going to want to hear."

"I suppose I could come back for a day or two for that."

He touched her lips to silence her, then found himself wanting to replace his fingertips with his mouth. She was so lush and sweet, and he needed to know that she'd really forgiven him for his sins. But that wouldn't be fair to her. He maintained a slight distance between his body and hers.

"There's more," he whispered.

"More clients coming?"

"More I want you to do."

"Griffin," she said against his fingertips, and he heard how shallow and strained her breathing was. For her sake and his he released her.

"It isn't fair to ask this," he said, "but…"

"Ask."

"Casey told me he wishes he could do the things you do. He's completely entranced with the gardens. I was hoping you might help him to make one that's all his own. Flowers, maybe some vegetables, too."

"Did he ask you to ask me?"

"No, and I didn't mention it to him. I didn't want to put you on the spot or promise him things he couldn't have. If I got him all excited about it, and then things didn't work out…"

She smiled up at him then, a weak smile but a warm one. "Have I told you yet today that you're an extremely good father?"

He just shook his head. "I just love him. Any man or woman who loves a child and wants them to be happy will do anything they can to make it so. But he doesn't know I've asked this of you, Abby, so you have a choice."

She chuckled and shook her head slowly. "No, I don't."

"You do."

"No. I want him to be happy, too. And you know what? I would love to make a garden with Casey."

"You'll stay, then?" He did his best not to touch her

again, though every cell in his body was directing him to kiss her.

"This won't take long," she warned. "A few days at best."

"I know."

And he knew she would go then. For good. She wouldn't want to continue to see him. She had her own child and her own future to think of, and he was just complicating things for her. He had to let her go.

"Don't worry about Cheryl," he told her as she turned to leave, knowing that no matter what he said, she would worry. And so would he. Cheryl was going to do her best to take Casey from him, and he wasn't sure that all his money and power could make a difference. In some cases and in some judges' courtrooms, being wealthy might work against him.

"Griffin?"

He looked into her eyes, and she turned back and rose on her toes. Lightly she pressed her lips against his cheek, and he breathed in the soft soapy scent of her.

"Thank you for caring enough to send a bodyguard. Don't do it again, though."

He wouldn't, but he would continue to worry. How on earth was he going to stop worrying about her once he was back in Chicago and she was here with another man?

Chapter Eleven

The last three days had been good, Abby admitted, as she and Casey lay against some pillows on the floor, staring at the pictures in the seed catalog. At least as good as they could be, considering the things she didn't want to think about.

"How 'bout those? I like those," Casey said, pointing to a tropical plant with gorgeous pink flowers.

"Very pretty," Abby agreed, not wanting to give him the bad news that the poor plant could never withstand Illinois winters. "But look at this one. What do you think? It only blooms at night. Kind of like a vampire."

"It's a vampire plant?"

"To most people it's a moonflower," she whispered, "but you and me? We know its secret. To us, it's a vampire plant. How about it? Should we plant some of these?"

"Dad! Dad!," Casey said, getting up and running with the catalog. "Look! See! Abby and me is growing vampire fwowers."

"I see," Griffin said with a laugh, and Abby looked up to see him enter the room. He gazed down to where she had kicked off her shoes, her bare legs exposed, and she realized that he really *did* see. Usually she wore jeans or even maternity overalls to hide her swelling stomach and make it easier to kneel in the dirt, but today had been especially hot, and she and Casey had simply been in the planning stages, so she had indulged herself with a pair of white shorts.

"Don't move," Griffin whispered as she struggled to rise to bring less attention to her bare skin. "You're fine just as you are." His eyes shone dark silver, and Abby felt a shiver of desire arc through her body.

"They're not really vampires, Casey, you know," she said, realizing that she enjoyed having Griffin stare at her too much.

"I know. Moonfwowers, but they're like vampires," Casey added. "You said."

"And they are," she added. "They're very cool."

"We're growing vampire fwowers, Dad," Casey repeated.

"Well, if anyone can make vampire flowers grow, it's Abby," Griffin said.

"Griffin, are you there?" Cheryl's voice suddenly sounded in the kitchen. It was obvious that she'd let herself in.

"Here, Mom," Casey called, and the sound of footsteps echoed on the old wooden floors.

Abby hopped up and nearly stumbled in her haste. Griffin caught her by the arm.

"Steady," he said. "You're fine. You're right where you should be." And he held on to her until she was firmly balanced, even though Cheryl had already entered the room and was staring at them pointedly. ''Something I can help you with, Cheryl?''

''Not really. I was just wondering if you were here. I came to see Casey.''

Griffin nodded.

''Me and Abby are growin' fwowers,'' Casey said. ''We got a book.'' And he pointed to the catalog Abby was holding.

Abby started to hold it out to him, but he shook his head. ''You show Mom the vampire ones.''

Cheryl blinked. Abby started to explain, but the woman shook her head. ''I'm sure there's a story behind all this.''

''Abby's a fine landscaper, Cheryl,'' Griffin said. ''And she's graciously agreed to stay on longer and help Casey plant his own garden even though it wasn't in the original plans.'' His tone brooked no argument.

''I'm sure she has,'' Cheryl said, her voice cool. ''Well, I won't get in her way. Plan away,'' she said. ''I'll just watch you and my son.''

And for five whole minutes that's what she did, until the telephone rang in the distance and Mrs. Digner came to get Griffin. ''I'm sorry, but it's Chicago,'' she said.

He frowned. ''Tell them I'll call them back.''

Cheryl gave a long sigh. ''I won't eat her while you're gone,'' she said, ''and I won't leave with anything that doesn't belong to me.'' Abby watched as the woman gave an imperceptible nod toward Casey.

Griffin gave a short bark of laughter. ''I'd like to see you try to eat Abby. She might surprise you.''

Abby blushed and pretended to be interested in the catalog.

''You eat people, Mom?'' Casey asked as his father left the room.

And Abby was surprised by the vulnerable, warm smile that suffused Cheryl's face. "Not lately," she promised her son. "Come on, show me what you're going to plant." And as he fetched the catalog, she took him on her lap and wrapped her arms around him, resting her chin on the top of his soft hair. She murmured appreciative comments as he pointed to the plants that he liked best.

Abby started to make a quiet exit.

"Not yet," Cheryl said quietly, and Abby looked up to see the woman looking at her. "Please," she said, although it sounded more like a command than a request.

"All right," Abby said. "Casey's a very promising gardener."

"Is that right, big guy?" Cheryl asked, ruffling her son's hair. "You show me your stuff."

Casey nodded, and Cheryl gave Abby a questioning look.

So Abby sat. She pretended to look at the other catalogs she had, but in truth she noticed everything that went on between mother and son. Cheryl oohed and aahed at all the right places. She hugged Casey several times. In spite of her silk blouse and white linen pants, she even got down on the ground with him when he got tired of looking at the catalogs and consented to a game of Candyland, which she managed to lose, even though she had been on a clear road to a win.

Eventually, though, Casey got tired and his mother took him off for a nap. "I'd like to talk," she said to Abby before she left the room.

When she returned, the smile she'd had for Casey was gone. "My son likes you," she said, "and that bears weight with his father. It bears weight with me, too, because I pay close attention to his companions, but it won't matter in the end. I want to make one thing clear, and that is this—I don't want Casey to get attached to you. Listen carefully and well. I don't know what you're after, but Griffin isn't going to marry you, no matter how nice he is and no matter how badly you need a husband. Don't even start having those kinds of thoughts.''

Abby almost gasped, but she managed to catch herself. She crossed her arms. ''How do you know?'' she asked. If Cheryl wanted to play this game, she would get a worthy opponent.

''I think I've made my reasons clear before. Griffin doesn't do domesticity. I've told you that several times.''

''And yet I haven't heeded your warnings.''

Cheryl leaned closer, right into Abby's personal space. ''Let me make myself even clearer, then. You may have a way with children, but I won't have Griffin bringing his…his women into my son's life.''

''What about Stuart?''

For a minute Abby thought Cheryl might strike her. The woman bared her teeth, lightning flashed in her eyes. Abby steeled herself for the blow, but she didn't step away.

''You have a lot of nerve, lady,'' Cheryl said. ''What about Stuart?''

Abby drew herself up to her full height and studied Cheryl closely. ''Didn't you bring Stuart into Casey's life? Did you ask for Griffin's approval?''

Cheryl narrowed her eyes. ''That is completely different. My relationship with Stuart would never hurt anyone.''

And then something became completely clear to

Abby. Cheryl hadn't said that Stuart's relationship with her would never hurt *Casey.* She had said it would never hurt *anyone.*

A sharp, undefined pain sliced through Abby, making it hard to breathe or speak. She studied Cheryl for long seconds. "How could I have missed it?" she whispered, horrified at the truth that beat at her. "You're still in love with him."

"What?" Cheryl's face grew ashen. She drew back. Footsteps sounded in the hallway. Abby heard them, but mostly she heard the accusation echoing through her mind.

"You're still in love with Griffin, and that's why you want to take Casey from him. To punish him." She whispered the words, half to herself, and yet it was clear that Cheryl had heard every word.

"I dumped Griffin, not the other way around."

"Lots of people walk away from the ones they love when it gets to be too painful."

The room went silent, except for a man clearing his throat. Stuart stood in the doorway. It was obvious that he had heard the pertinent parts of the conversation.

"Stuart," Cheryl cried out. She looked at her husband, her face parchment pale. Stuart's eyes rested on her with deep sadness.

Instantly regret washed through Abby. "I'm...I'm sorry," she said. "Please forget I said that."

But her words went unanswered. Cheryl moved quickly to her husband's side, sending Abby one angry, anguished look. Quickly and quietly the pair left. The silence was as heavy as any Abby had ever known.

She watched out the window as Cheryl and Stuart neared the car. For a minute they stood looking at each other. Then Cheryl threw herself into her husband's arms, visibly sobbing. Abby noted the gentle way Stuart held his wife as she cried. She noted how Cheryl turned to him. She remembered how Cheryl had been with Casey today, her feelings for him so obvious, and she wondered how Cheryl could be so loving to her child and yet not see how badly she would hurt Casey if she tried to keep him from his father.

Mixed emotions filled her soul. She didn't like harming others, and she had clearly done that by her careless words.

As Abby looked out the window again and watched Cheryl and Stuart drive away, she wondered how Griffin would feel about her now that she'd opened the doors and invited ten more kinds of trouble into his world.

Surely there was a limit to how much pain he could take from her.

There was definitely a limit to how much pain she would allow herself to wittingly inflict on the man she loved.

The truth hit hard. Abby took a deep breath and concentrated on trying to push that thought back into the deep hole in her soul where it had been hiding.

But there was no running from the hard facts anymore.

All she could do was run from Griffin.

"I have to go now." Griffin heard Abby say the words. He registered the determination in her voice, and he knew that she wasn't just referring to the fact that she was leaving for the day.

"No." His response was automatic, as much a part of him as anything had ever been.

She turned tortured blue eyes to him. "There's really no reason for me to be here."

"I hired you to do a job."

"And I've done it. We both know that this last business with Casey was merely make-work. I can order all the plants for him, and there are a hundred people in the area that you can appeal to for help. This is farm country, Griffin. People know how to put seeds in the ground."

He opened his mouth to speak.

She held up her hand. "And don't tell me that you need me to be here to explain to your clients what every tree and shrub is. I've been in this business for years. Very few people are interested in the details. If anyone is, I'll leave some of my cards. You can send them my way."

She was squelching all of his arguments. He was having trouble coming up with new ones. There were real reasons why he didn't want her to go, but she wouldn't want to hear those. She wouldn't want to know that he simply wanted her near him. He felt as if the very life was running out of his body.

"Don't go," he said.

"I have to. And I have to tell you something, too. Today the reason that Cheryl and Stuart left so suddenly was no accident. Cheryl and I had words."

Griffin frowned. He moved closer. She backed away.

He swore beneath his breath. "Dammit, Abby, I'm not going to hurt you."

She stopped and stood her ground. "You think I don't know that? You don't think I know that you've been very, very careful never to hurt me? I know that, Griffin. I'm grateful that you've kept your distance. I've made it clear that I'm susceptible to your charms, and I thank you for not pushing those boundaries.''

His hands half-reaching out to her, he stopped his forward progress and closed his eyes. What was a man supposed to say to something like that?

''To hell with boundaries,'' he said, but he didn't step closer. He couldn't force himself on her.

She shook her head. ''I found out something today. Your wife…your ex-wife is still in love with you.''

And that caught him off balance. He looked at her with disbelief. ''Cheryl?''

She tried a smile, even though she failed miserably. ''You have other ex-wives I should know about, cowboy?''

''Just the one, but I can guarantee that you're wrong on that count. Cheryl isn't in love with me.''

''I'm sure she is.''

''She wasn't even in love with me when we got married.''

''You probably thought that was the truth.''

''It was. That wasn't why we married. I wanted a helper, and she wanted a man who could offer her security. She did her part, I didn't do mine. But love wasn't in the picture for either of us.''

''Maybe you don't know what love looks like.''

Maybe he didn't, but he knew that his heart was ripping in two just looking at Abby. If she would only let him near….

He took a step forward, and she looked so scared that he stopped. Using all of his willpower, he forced himself to keep his distance.

''Abby, maybe I don't know exactly what you're talking about, but I know one thing. Cheryl isn't shy. If she loved me, she would have said so.''

''Maybe she will, now that I've told her that I know her secret.'' Abby blushed a lovely deep rose. She twisted her fingers against each other. She looked up at him with a pain so deep in her eyes that Griffin was sure he could see straight into her soul.

''Abby,'' he drawled. ''Sweetheart, don't look that way.''

''I can't help it. My being here is creating problems. Cheryl may be married to Stuart, but she's obviously in love with you. That's why she's trying to take Casey from you. I just— I can't stay. That's only adding fuel to the fire.''

''You're not doing anything wrong.''

She turned her face slightly away. ''Yes. I am. I'm hurting.'' She turned farther away. ''I can't...I don't want to stay here any longer.''

And nothing in the world, not logic or sympathy or a stampeding herd of wild ex-wives could keep him from Abby's side right then. If she was hurting, if he was doing that to her, then it was as clear as anything had ever been clear, that he had to let her go, to set her free.

But he couldn't let her stand here and suffer without trying to offer her some comfort. That just wasn't a possibility.

He moved forward, resting his hands on the mantelpiece she was standing next to, gazing down at her.

''I would never hurt you,'' he promised. ''I couldn't knowingly do that. It would be unforgivable.''

And she twisted from her position, looking up at him with misty eyes. ''You're not the one hurting me. I am. I outed Cheryl, and now she's going to come after you and Casey. How can I live with that?''

He shook his head, tucked one finger beneath her chin. ''You didn't do a thing wrong.''

''Except what I always do. I went in headfirst and stopped to think later. No woman is going to suffer that kind of humiliation and not do something about it. She'll try to take him.''

''She's tried before.''

''Every time I try to help, I end up hurting you.''

''No.'' He bent and kissed her just beneath the jawline.

''Yes.'' She kissed him on the chin.

And that was all he needed. He grasped her by the forearms and pulled her close. He covered her mouth with his and tasted the salt of her tears and the sweetness that was hers alone.

She rose on her toes and pressed closer.

His head spun. He speared his fingers through the softness of her hair. ''Abby…sweet, brave Abby…stay,'' he whispered. ''Stay.''

And she broke away with a cry. ''Look at me. Just look at me. I'm trying to do the right thing, and I'm doing the wrong thing. This is bad. This is me making a mistake all over again, being weak. I don't want to be weak, Griffin. I have to leave. If I do, maybe you'll fix things up with Cheryl, and everything will be all right. But for sure if I stay, everything is just going to go more wrong. I…thank you for hiring me. It was…it was—''

''It was the best move I ever made,'' he whispered, still folded around her.

She bit her lip, moving slightly. He felt her skin slide against his, and he wanted to pull her close and hold her, but he could see the pain in her eyes.

Griffin stepped back and let her go.

"Goodbye, Griffin," she said. "Tell Casey…tell him to water the vampire plants, and tell him he's a wonderful gardener."

And then she practically ran from him. He followed her out onto the porch, and she flew to her truck. For two seconds she stumbled on the grass and he started to rush down the stairs, but she held up one hand and shook her head.

He let her go, fearing that if he tried to go near her, he would make her more frantic and she would end up getting hurt or the baby would, which would absolutely kill her.

For just two quick seconds she looked back at him when she entered her truck.

And he did his best to memorize her face and every line of her body. He tried to imprint everything there was of her on his soul.

Then she was gone.

Griffin looked around. He gazed at the maze and the trees and shrubs and the pink and gold and blue flowers that she had left behind. She was here, all around. The fragrance of her art scented the warm summer air, lingering like footprints in wet sand.

But Abby herself was gone from his life. He knew that he wouldn't see her again.

And a cry began deep within him. He had handled his relationships with women badly before. This time, though, he wondered if he would ever recover from his loss.

Chapter Twelve

The bell hanging above the shop door jangled, and Abby forced herself to look up. It had been four days since she had run from Griffin's house, and she was barely hanging on. But she was determined to make it look as if she was handling everything just fine. Business as usual. She kept her hands in the soil she had placed in the forest-green pot.

Delia walked in the door. In her wake came Lydia and Sunny, Joyce and Evangelina, Ellie Donahue and Mercy Granahan, Rosellen January and a good half dozen other women. They came in all shapes and sizes, all different hair colors, and a multitude of clothing styles. The one thing they all had in common today was the look in their eyes. Abby knew what that look meant, and she intended to ignore it.

''Somebody die at the café?'' she asked. ''I have a pot of coffee in the back, but comparing it to Lydia's would be like comparing swamp water to fresh. Still, it will keep your eyes open if that's what you need.''

''You know we're not here for coffee,'' Delia said, her voice small and scared.

Abby knew. She and Delia had been working in close quarters for the past few days, Delia chattering away while Abby couldn't manage to let go of her silence.

''I know,'' Abby acknowledged. ''I'm sorry if I scared you. I'll try to be more communicative.''

''If you have to try, then something's wrong,'' Sunny pointed out. ''What did that man do to you?''

''What man?'' Somehow Abby managed to get the words past the huge lump in her throat. She made a desperate attempt not to think of the man Sunny was referring to.

''Honey...'' Lydia began in that mother-hen voice of hers that nearly broke Abby's composure completely. Lydia had a big doughy body made for comfort, and it would be so easy to rest there for a while, Abby thought, to let the tears fall. Except that once she let the tears begin, she was afraid she'd never be able to stop them. And besides, if she cried, someone was sure to say something to Griffin, if they didn't clout him upside the head. And if anyone told, then he would know her secret. She just couldn't let that happen, especially since absolutely none of this was any of his fault.

She was the idiotic one who had gone and fallen hopelessly, terribly, completely in love with a man she could never have. She knew with a certainty that this time there was no getting over the man, either. She was going to have to live with this pain for a long time. It would be easier to do that if he didn't know how she felt.

Abby took a deep breath. She even tried a small smile. ''I'm not sure what you're all thinking, but I'm perfectly fine, just a little tired. It happens to pregnant women, you know.'' She heard Sunny's snort and gave her friend a defiant look.

''Don't go looking at me that way, Abby,'' Sunny said. ''You know we didn't come over here to cause you grief.''

Abby let out a sigh. ''I know, and really, I appreciate the fact that you want to help me, but—'' she struggled against the tears that threatened ''—but you know how I am. I'm used to going it alone. If I lean, I'll topple, and I just couldn't bear that. It's easier to keep pushing on the way I am.''

''Oh, Abby,'' Mercy said. ''We don't want you to feel so alone.''

''You know we love you,'' Joyce said. ''That man…I could just—''

Alarm coursed through Abby. ''There is no man,'' she said sternly. ''And if you love me, you'll abide by that.''

Her statement brought about a lot of grumbling and shuffling from her friends.

''But, for the record, I love all of you, too.'' Abby nearly muttered the words. ''I'm sorry if I haven't said so before. Speaking my feelings doesn't come easily to me.''

''Oh, Abby, we know it. Just as long as you know that we're here for you if you need us,'' Rosellen said, and the tall, skinny woman came behind the counter and put her arms around Abby.

Abby hugged her back, and soon the tiny space behind the counter was filled with women hugging and patting hair and comforting.

Until Lydia turned and looked out the window. ''There's Griffin,'' she said.

And a silence fell on the flower shop. The entire

group of women turned toward the window, all except Abby. She took one sideways glance at Griffin, who stood there face forward, staring at her. It was all she could do to keep from leaping over the counter and running out the door to launch herself into his arms. Instead, she turned back to the forest-green pot. She knew when Griffin had moved on by the way every woman in the store relaxed suddenly.

"Thank you all for coming by," she said as cheerfully as she could muster. "But as you can see, I'm just fine."

"Abby," Delia said, moving closer. "Whatever are you going to do?" And the young woman looked down at Abby's growing belly.

"What am I going to do?" Abby asked, hoping her voice didn't sound too fragile. "I'm going to pot this azalea."

And then she was going to go tell Thomasina that she was no longer interested in finding a man of any kind. Ever.

Some things just couldn't be fixed. Griffin knew that. It was a tenet he lived by. Part of the reason he was so successful in business was because he knew when to forge ahead, when a problem could be worked around, and when he just had to let go.

He'd made his fortune living by those rules.

This was one of those problems that appeared to be unfixable. There weren't going to be any winners in this game. He was losing Abby. No, that wasn't right. He had already lost her, he reminded himself, remembering how she had pointedly looked away from him when he'd seen her through the glass of the florist. She didn't want anything to do with him, any more than she wanted Lucius Alloway.

He had to accept that, had to ignore the empty place in his heart, the urge to run down the street and enter her store if only to hear her say his name once more.

Going near her wasn't allowed. She had said that being with him hurt her. He damn well wasn't going to hurt her, but he was at least going to fix one or two problems that were worrying her. He could at least ease her mind a bit, because Abby was right about one thing. He had been punishing himself for what he'd done and failed to do in the past, and by punishing himself, he was setting up a scenario where Casey could be hurt all over again. That just wasn't going to happen.

So, much as he hated the thought of entering into another argument with Cheryl, Griffin found himself walking into the Red Rose Heaven Hotel and knocking on his ex-wife's hotel room door.

Stuart opened the door.

Griffin nodded. "Hello, Stuart. I'm sorry to barge in this way, but I have a few things I need to discuss with your wife. I would appreciate it if you'd stick around. This is for your ears, too."

"Sure, Griff, come on in." He gestured toward a chair in the sitting area. "I'll just get Cheryl." But Cheryl came through the door at that minute. She was carrying her purse.

"Griffin, we were just coming to see you," she said. Her voice was faint. Griffin was almost sure that was a slight blush on her face, though Cheryl had never been a blusher.

"Something important?" he asked. "Or were you coming to visit Casey? He's with Mrs. Digner right now. You can go there just as soon as we've talked."

“No. No, it was you I wanted to talk to this time. I—” She looked at her husband as if she couldn’t go on, then sank down onto the couch. Stuart took his place beside her and took her hand in his own.

“You’ve probably heard what happened at your house the other day,” Stuart said, which surprised Griffin. Usually when Stuart and Cheryl were in a room, she did all the talking. “When Abby declared that Cheryl was still in love with you, that came as quite a shock to me, but I wasn’t at all sure that she didn’t have it right.”

“You know that she didn’t,” Cheryl said, gazing up at her husband, a pleading expression in her eyes. “I love you, Stuart.”

And Stuart put his arm around his wife. “I know you do, honey. At least I know that now.” He turned toward Griffin. “I think I owe a debt of gratitude toward your Abby. She brought some things out in the open that needed to be addressed.”

Cheryl bit her lip. She looked at Griffin. “I guess she did, Griffin. When she insisted that I was still in love with you, I couldn’t believe what she was saying. That is, it’s not that you’re unlovable, Griff, but you… I…well, we never—”

Griffin held up his hand. He gave a low chuckle. “I’m not sure my ego can take too much of this, Cheryl, but yes, I told Abby the same thing. You and I never were in love.”

She gave a hard nod. “I was so scared that Stuart would see things the way she did, though, and when we got back here and began to talk, I realized why Abby had made that leap to thinking I was in love with you. When a woman spends this much time spewing hateful language toward her ex-husband and the women he is involved with, well I guess anyone might think that I was jealous. And you know what? She was right. I am jealous."

Griffin opened his eyes wide and shifted uncomfortably on the padded chair. "Cheryl..."

She shook her head. "I'm not jealous of Abby, and I'm not in love with you, Griffin. I've come off that way, because I was so afraid of losing Casey. You're a god among businessmen. You know a lot of powerful people. The one thing I had going for me was the fact that I was married and you weren't. I had more free time, I could tell people that I was providing a two-parent home where there would always be someone there. From the beginning I've been afraid that you might take him from me. I can see how much he loves you."

"Of course he loves me, Cheryl. I'm his father. And you're his mother. He loves you, too. I'll put that in writing if you'd like."

"Yes, but..."

"Cheryl, I would never try to separate you and Casey. Ever. He loves you, he needs you."

Tears ran down Cheryl's face. "It's just like you to be so logical and good about this when I've been doing my best to keep Casey from you. What will people think of me now?"

"They'll think you're a mother who is worried about losing her child. They'll understand."

"They will, honey," Stuart said. "Anyone can see that you love Casey to death."

"I love you, too, Stuart. I really do, even if that's not why I married you."

Stuart beamed in a way Griffin had never seen.

"About Abby," Griffin began.

"I'm going to apologize to her," Cheryl said. "My bad behavior put me in danger of losing my husband, and she was the one who woke me up. And for the record, Griffin, I'll be better about Casey from here on out. I know he needs you as much as he needs me."

"Too bad we always seem to be in different states," he said.

"That is too bad," Stuart said. "I guess some things just can't be fixed."

His words echoed Griffin's thoughts a few minutes earlier much too closely.

Griffin nodded as he got to his feet and held out his hand. "Somehow we'll make this work," he promised.

"Are you going to see Abby?" Cheryl asked.

"Eventually," he said. As if anything could stop him, now that he had news that would ease her suffering.

"We heard that she quit her job," Cheryl said. "I have to think that that's my fault. As I said, I'm going to go see her and apologize. Is there anything you'd like me to do or say?"

Griffin nodded tightly. "Yes, let me talk to her first. And pray for a miracle. This has nothing to do with you," he told his ex-wife when she started to apologize again. "What's gone wrong with Abby and me has been entirely my fault. I'm going to need a miracle to change that."

"I hope you find one," his ex-wife said softly as the door closed behind Griffin. He knew that Cheryl assumed that he was on his way to see Abby, but there was one other person he had to see first.

"I told you that I didn't want you to send me any more candidates for husband." Abby spoke into the telephone receiver.

"I know," Thomasina said, "but this one just got past me. I don't know where my head was when I was talking to him. Probably with Jeffrey Seeton. Did I tell you that he got so desperate to find a woman that he actually asked me out on a date?" Thomasina asked. "Of course I said no. I know he's the kind who just has one thing on his mind. I'm sure he was trying to look through my blouse the whole time I was interviewing him."

"Tommy, stop."

Thomasina stopped. "I'm sorry, we were talking about your date."

"Yes, you were trying to explain why you were still sending me dates when I'd specifically asked you not to. Did Jeffrey Seeton really ask you out?"

Tommy practically twittered as she admitted that the matchmaker had a man trying to match up with her.

"Good. So we're agreed then that you're not sending any more men."

"Right, just as soon as you meet this one."

"Not even one, Tommy."

"Oh. I'm sorry. I'm afraid I can't do anything about this one. He's already on his way over to your house."

"He's what?" Abby squawked. "Tommy, you promised..."

"I know, but he really wanted to date you, and—"

The doorbell rang. Tommy apparently heard it. "I'll talk to you later, Abby. Just remember to say no to anything you really don't want to do. That almost always works."

Abby put the phone back on the hook. She felt a headache coming on, and a backache, and she wondered where Griffin was with his bodyguards and his easy smile that made her heart hurt. She did not want to open the door. Tommy had never sent a man to her house before. It might not be safe. She had a baby to think about. Maybe she should call Griffin and have him come over just to make sure the man didn't get out of line.

And the very thought nearly brought tears to her eyes. She couldn't call Griffin. For anything. She would have to tough this out alone, just as she would have to face everything for the rest of her life. Alone.

Without any more thought, Abby yanked the door open. ''I'm sorry, but Tommy made a mistake. The position of husband isn't open anymore.''

''It's not?'' The familiar male voice drifted in, and Abby blinked her eyes and focused on the man standing before her. Tall, lean and dark-haired with silver eyes that filled her with longing, Griffin O'Dell was holding out a bouquet of peach-colored roses.

''Griffin? Why are you here?'' she asked, her voice a high-pitched whisper. Abby suddenly became aware of the fact that she was wearing cutoff denim shorts that barely fastened over her belly, an old T-shirt that declared that she was ''Hell on Wheels'' and no shoes or makeup. No point in putting on mascara when a woman was just going to cry it off.

She looked down at the flowers he still held.

He shifted uncomfortably. ''Delia came through in a pinch,'' he said.

''You brought me flowers?'' she asked, unable to keep the wonder from her voice. ''No one has ever brought me flowers. I guess when you're the flower lady, they figure there's no need.''

''I felt...a need,'' he said simply. ''Is it true that you're done husband hunting?'' His voice sounded strange, un-Griffin-like.

Abby nodded slowly. ''I'm done.'' She took the flowers and buried her nose in them. She tried to still her thundering heart. ''Is something wrong with Casey? Can I help?'' The sudden thought that something might have happened to the little boy filled her with panic. She looked up at Griffin, unable to keep the worry from her eyes.

''He's fine, Abby. But he misses you.''

''Oh.''

''Yes, definitely 'oh.'''

''I miss him, too.''

''But Casey's not the problem.''

''Okay,'' Abby managed to say. ''So Casey's not why you're here. Maybe there's a problems with the gardens,'' she ventured. ''Is that why you're here?''

He shook his head slowly. His eyes grew darker, his gaze more intent.

''When a man brings a woman flowers, Abby, he usually has something specific in mind.''

Her heart started to trip. ''Half the time when men bring flowers, it's because they've done something they're sorry for and they're trying to fix things, but that wouldn't be you.''

A trace of amusement curved his lips. ''Don't be so sure, Abby. I've done many things wrong lately. I'm hoping to fix that. Heard from Tommy lately?''

She fought for breath. ''Yes, she said she was sending me a date. I told her not to, but it was too late.''

''Was it?''

''Oh, yes. I told you I—''

''You no longer need a husband.''

''That's right.'

''Is that because— Abby, does that mean you've already found a man to marry? Maybe one you found on your own?'' His voice came out hoarse and raw.

Her heart raced faster. ''No,'' she whispered. ''I just decided that I couldn't marry anyone.''

''No one?''

''No. The day after I left you, I almost called Tommy and told her I would reconsider Lucius.''

Griffin let out a low growl.

''I know. It was just desperation. I realized I was becoming reckless.''

Griffin smiled. He reached out and touched her hair, and it was all she could do not to turn her face into the palm of his hand. ''You were born reckless, Abby. You risk being heard talking to inanimate objects. You make pacts with matchmakers. You brave angry ex-wives. Your recklessness is one of your most endearing traits, but I'm glad you passed on Lucius. He's not for you.''

''No. No one is.'' Which was, oh, so hard to say when she wanted him so much.

He tilted his head and studied her. ''I thought you might like to know that I talked to Cheryl.''

Abby did her best not to flinch. Was he going to tell her that Cheryl and Stuart were getting a divorce and he was going to marry her again?

''She told me that part of the reason she'd been fighting me so hard about Casey is that she was afraid I would get married. It seems that was the one advantage she thought she would have in the courts, the fact that she's married and I'm not.''

Abby nodded solemnly.

''I've been thinking she was right. I should get married and give Casey a more solid home,'' he said suddenly.

Her heart lurched so hard and so painfully that Abby

was afraid Griffin would notice. She could barely draw breath in and out of her body. She could barely keep from doubling over.

"You probably have a point," she managed to whisper. She felt the stems of the flowers crush beneath her fingers. "I know there are plenty of women in Red Rose who might suit. You probably know more elsewhere."

Slowly Griffin shook his head. He raised his hand and cupped her cheek. "I only know of one woman who would suit. You're it, Abby. That's why I'm here, flowers in hand."

It was all she could do not to turn into his touch, to rub her cheek against his skin, to touch her lips to his palm. "Oh…no," she said on a gasp. "The courts would probably take Casey away completely. There was that article, and…this," she said, glancing down at her belly, "and Cheryl would probably be completely ticked off."

"I think the courts would be delighted that Casey has two families to love him, and I don't think Cheryl will be a problem anymore. She wanted me to thank you for what you said the other day. It made her realize what she was risking by continuing to try to make things tough for Casey and me. She loves Stuart, you know. She was just afraid that I might marry and gain an edge in the battle for Casey. After some thought, she and Stuart have actually decided to settle in Red Rose, so that Casey can live here year-round. They've kind of fallen in love with the town, and Stuart's a plumber. He's been wanting to move away from the city for some time, and it seems that Red Rose could use a good plumber now that Ellie is getting married. They told me the news just before I came here. Cheryl's also willing to be more generous with my visitation rights. We'll share equally.''

''Then you can see Casey year-round, and you don't need a wife.''

Slowly Griffin shook his head. He moved closer. ''Oh, you are so wrong, Abby. I need a wife. I *want* a wife. Tommy is doing her best to help me. Haven't you guessed why I'm here yet, Abby?''

Abby's mind went numb. She didn't dare turn her thoughts in the direction they were trying to go.

''Abby, love, marry me.''

She wanted to say yes so badly, but she was afraid to even think that there was hope for her and Griffin. ''Oh, no, not me.''

He gazed directly into her eyes. He brushed her lips with his thumb. ''You and only you.''

''Why?'' She stood her ground. She would not go blindly into a relationship ever again. No doubt that meant that she would lose Griffin, because she realized that she couldn't marry a man simply for expedience...for either of them.

''Abby, you're the only woman for me, because you're the woman I love. The only woman I ever loved, the only woman I will ever love. If you can't love me, too—'' he tilted his head back, blinking, visibly swallowing ''—then at least let me be a father to your baby. Let me at least do what you would have asked of those other men you went to Tommy for.''

Abby closed her eyes as the tears slid in behind her lids. She blinked, then forced herself to stare into his eyes. ''How could you think that I couldn't love you?'' Her voice shook, but she got the words out.

Griffin raised his brows.

Abby frowned. ''I know what you're thinking, but I

never said I couldn't love you. I only said that we wouldn't suit. And I said that because you made me feel too much, and I was afraid of that. I knew you would never love me."

A smile lifted Griffin's lips then. "Oh, but I do, Abby. I hate to call you a liar, sweetheart, but I do love you. Completely. Be as stubborn as you like, argue with me if you must, but you can't stop me from loving you until the day I die."

And Abby's heart opened up. She threw her arms around Griffin's neck, her tears coming hard and fast. "I love you to distraction," she said. "And you are going to regret this moment of weakness so much."

"Oh, no. Never." And he kissed her, fast and hard, leaving her breathless and wanting more.

Pulling back slightly, she raised one brow and placed her hands on her hips. "May I remind you that I'm willful, outspoken and that I act without thinking at times?"

"Umm." He traced a lazy finger slowly across her mouth, then kissed her. "I know," he said when he raised his head. "And I absolutely adore those parts of you."

Abby's eyes widened. "You know all my worst traits and you still want me?"

His eyes turned dark and fierce. "I want all your worst traits, your best traits, I want every part of you. Right now I want your lips. Again." And he pulled her to him.

She stayed there in his arms, her forehead against his, her lips only a breath away. "I loved you from the start," she confessed with a soft smile. "It was like…magic. I couldn't help myself. I wonder if it was that Midas touch they say you possess."

He kissed the corner of her mouth. ''It was something much better. It was love. I felt it, too. Right from the start.''

And at that moment Abby's baby kicked. She looked up at Griffin, who was grinning. ''I hope that meant, 'Welcome, Dad,''' he said.

''I'm sure it did,'' she said with a laugh.

''Casey is going to be so excited,'' he added. ''A second mom, and one he loves already.''

''Well, that's good, because I absolutely adore him, too,'' she said.

''I suppose you know I'm staying in Red Rose. It's home for us now,'' he whispered.

''Are you sure?'' She looked up, a trace of uncertainty in her voice.

He whirled her around slowly, giving her a long, luscious kiss. ''Are you kidding? Red Rose is our home now. We found what we were looking for. You, Abby, my love. And you, too, baby O'Dell-to-be.'' And he lifted Abby high and kissed her stomach before gently lowering her to her feet.

''Let's go tell Tommy,'' he said.

''This is going to break her heart,'' Abby warned. ''She likes to make the matches around here.''

''Who knows? Maybe she did. Somehow I still can't believe that Tommy set you up with Lucius Alloway. I have a pretty good feeling that she knew I was going to be incredibly jealous,'' Griffin confessed.

''And that I was going to go running into your arms,'' Abby agreed with a startled gasp. ''Tommy sure makes good matches, doesn't she?''

''I couldn't have found a better match if I had searched a lifetime, love,'' Griffin said. ''Remind me to pay the lady a hefty commission. Later. For now, let's go home and start getting ready for our wedding.''

And he lifted Abby in his arms.

Abby shrieked. ''Griffin, what are you doing? I'm getting big as a house, and it shows. I'm so heavy. Put me down.''

Griffin laughed as he carried her outside and down the steps. ''Are you arguing with me, Abby?''

''Yes, I believe I am.''

''Good. Keep doing that. I love it when you argue. And for the record, I'm practicing carrying my bride over the threshold. I intend to do it very soon, long before our son or daughter gets here.''

Abby suddenly sat still in his arms. ''Our son or daughter. Oh, Griffin, this baby will be ours, won't it?''

''No one else's, lady. Just as you'll be no other man's. Make sure that Tommy knows that, won't you?''

''I think she already knows,'' Abby said, gesturing toward where Griffin's car was parked. Tommy was there, waving. On the back window, she had written in soap, ''Just Engaged.''

''Another satisfied customer,'' she said with a smile as they drew close.

''Two satisfied customers,'' Griffin corrected her, as he set Abby down gently. ''Close your eyes, Tommy. I'm going to kiss my bride-to-be.''

''Oh, please do,'' Tommy said. ''Just let me record this for my scrapbook of matches made.'' And she pulled a disposable camera from her purse.

Griffin, however, didn't appear to be listening. He took Abby into his arms and lowered his lips to hers. And Abby understood what everyone meant when they said that he had the Midas touch. His mouth on hers stole her breath and her thoughts. It changed her in indefinably lovely ways.

"That was a golden moment," she whispered when he pulled away. Everyone was right. "You have the touch."

"I was thinking the same thing about you," he said, still holding her close.

"Maybe we'd better try that again, then," she said. "Just to find out who's making the magic."

"I'd have to say that we are. Together."

"You're right. This only happens with you," she whispered. And then she rose on her toes and kissed the man she loved with all her heart, as the camera clicked off picture after picture.

* * * * *

Myrna's
BRIDES OF RED ROSE
trilogy continues!

Don't miss
THE BLACK KNIGHT'S BRIDE
by Myrna Mackenzie

Susanna Wright has vowed to be no man's damsel in distress, but when she's stranded on the road, it's Brady Malone who comes to her rescue. Brady knows he's a no-good loner, he's always played the villain in town, but Susanna is determined to show him he's the only hero she'll ever need.

Coming only to Silhouette Romance in June 2004

For a sneak preview of this romantic story, just turn the page.

Chapter One

''We're okay, sweetie. Don't worry. We're all right.'' Susanna Wright tried to steer the limping car into the soft gravel at the side of the road and almost managed to do that before the car gave its last wheeze. She heard the hint of desperation in her voice as she whispered the words to her twelve-month-old daughter, Grace, sleeping soundly in the back seat. She wanted to wish for a miracle, but suppressed the desire. Miracles didn't tend to come her way. At least they hadn't for a long time.

''We're fine,'' she said again. Maybe Grace didn't need the reassurance, but Susanna did. The sky had already gone dark, they hadn't reached their destination, and she didn't know what was wrong with the car. Worse than that, there didn't seem to be much of anything out here except for a glow from one small house sitting about thirty feet off the road. Who knew what she'd find if she banged on the door of that house? And what if she didn't like what she found there? With a broken car, a baby and two miles of seemingly unlit road between her and her destination, the town of Red Rose, Illinois, just where would she run to? Better to just lie low here in the car and wait until morning.

She had just turned from taking her sleeping daughter from the car seat and settled her into her arms when something hit the roof of her car with a thump.

Susanna shrieked and pulled her baby tighter.

Grace started to cry.

The something that had landed on her car scratched away at the cloth top and then leapt off, hustling into the dark in the direction of the lighted house.

Almost immediately a barking and snarling began. The sound of metal clattering added to the noise, and the barking grew more frantic, deep-throated and threatening.

Suddenly light flooded the yard in front of the house. A tall man stepped outside.

"Stay, Scrap. Be still," he said in a voice as low and calm as any Susanna had ever heard. "Let's see what you have there." He bent on one knee and shined a light under the porch. "Just a raccoon, Scrap, probably trying to get into the garbage can. Drive you nuts, don't they? Come on into the house for a few minutes. It's not going to leave until you do, and you're not going to be quiet until it's gone."

The dog kept barking, the sound harsh and belligerent.

"Scrap," the man commanded in a lower, sterner voice.

The dog whimpered once, then subsided.

In the silence Grace let out a lusty cry.

Scrap barked again.

The flashlight swung in an arc, illuminating the car,

trapping Susanna in its beam. Her breath lodged in her chest somewhere, hurting her, but she couldn't let it out.

She couldn't see the man for the glare of the light now shining in her face, but she could hear his quiet command to his dog to stay, and she could hear his footsteps crunching on the ground as he moved nearer. The light of the flashlight bounced a bit, but remained on her face as she finally dragged air into her lungs in a shaky breath. The windows were closed, the car doors were locked, but she remembered her first glimpse of the man when he'd emerged from the house. He was tall with linebacker shoulders. A flimsy car window wouldn't be a match for him.

Slowly she started to edge over to the passenger seat, but she bumped up against Grace's car carrier, which she had moved there after they had stopped. It effectively blocked her way.

The footsteps came closer.

"Ma'am?" the man asked.

She didn't answer.

"Are you all right in there?" he added.

She considered maintaining her silence, but to what purpose? If she didn't say anything, he would, no doubt, keep moving closer.

"I—we're fine," she managed to get out. "We just stopped to rest. We'll be going in a minute. Now, actually." With Grace still on her lap, Susanna turned the key, praying that the few minutes of down time had been enough to fix whatever had been wrong. She didn't like leaving Grace unbelted, but at the moment the man seemed the larger threat to her child's safety. She would fasten her baby in properly once they were out of his sight.

But though she tried several times, the engine would

not turn over, and Susanna realized her mistake then. Both she and the man knew she had no way out of here.

"I don't think that car is going anywhere, ma'am," the man said quietly, but she noticed that he backed away a step. The slight gesture helped her breathe just a bit easier.

She pulled the key out of the ignition and struggled for composure. "Could you—would you be able to call a tow truck in town?"

"Not a problem." He pulled a portable phone from his pocket and started to move forward.

"No," she said, too suddenly, not wanting him to get that close. "You—you're from around here. You probably know the right place to call. Could you do it?"

There was a pause. She wished she was the one holding the light so she could see his expression, but he finally moved and punched in a number. He hit a button and she could hear the ringing, but there was no answer.

He dialed another number. "Ms. Woolverton, there's a stranded lady that needs a tow out at Malone Woods," he said. Susanna noted that he didn't identify himself in any way, and his voice was devoid of expression. He listened for what seemed like a long time. "Then when someone is available," he said and severed the connection.

"It might be some time," he told Susanna.

She took a deep breath. "We'll be fine. I—could I ask you—there's a hotel in town, the Red Rose Heaven, but I couldn't get a room when I called up earlier. Is there another place I could try?"

"No. No other place, and you're right about not being able to get a room at the Red Rose now. The town is crawling with strangers this weekend. A festival or something. Full.''

She nodded. She hadn't really wanted to stay at the hotel, anyway. The prices were higher than she could safely afford. None of this was working out the way she had dreamed when she had first read the reprinted story from the *Red Rose Gazette* on the Internet. A town with lots of women and very few men, a place where she would just be another female among many, a place so different from her own big city background that no one would think to look for her there.

Initially, her thoughts had just been musings, far-fetched daydreams in which she arrived in Red Rose in broad daylight, found some way to set herself up and got a job. Any job. She hadn't meant to actually do any of those things, but then Trent, her ex-husband, had shown up at her door. As if they hadn't been divorced for a year. He'd been doing that a lot lately, and each time had been ugly, frightening, even though he'd never physically threatened her. This time was worse. He had intimated that he had changed his mind about never wanting Grace. He had spun several scenarios where he could coerce Susanna into taking him back, making her feel cornered, knowing there was nothing she could really do to keep him away. At least nothing truly effective. He had the money and the influence to do lots of things. Trent knew people, and some of them might actually help him. He might try to take Grace for real, if only for spite or to force Susanna to come back to him.

And suddenly scared in a way she hadn't been before, Susanna was throwing things in her car and heading down the road with no destination in mind until her thoughts had cleared out just a bit, and she'd pointed the car in this direction. Now, here she was, in a dark, deserted place far outside the town, facing a strange man more than a head taller than Trent.

"Ma'am, your baby's crying."

Susanna took a deep breath to keep from crying, too. "I just have to feed her." She relaxed somewhat when she realized that he wasn't moving any closer to the car.

"Can I give you a lift into town, miss?" He said the words gently but without enthusiasm, as if he was as exasperated by the situation as she was.

And get into the car with a strange man? Possibly put Grace into greater danger?

"We'll be fine," she said, realizing that the phrase was fast becoming her mantra. "If we could just stay here in the car until the tow truck comes..."

The light bounced as if he had nodded. He didn't bother inviting her into his house, and she wondered if he didn't want her there or if he simply realized she wouldn't accept. "That's fine," he said in that deep, gritty voice. He started to turn back toward his house. "Come, Scrap," he said, and his tone held a note of affection. She supposed it had been there all along, but her fear had prevented her from noting it before.

"Thank you, Mr.—" She hesitated. He didn't fill in the blank. "I'm sorry, but I don't know your name," she said.

He stopped in his tracks, but he didn't turn around. "Malone," he said, his voice clipped, and then he started walking again.

"Thank you, Mr. Malone."

She watched him as he returned to his house. He walked with a slight limp, but an economy of movement otherwise, very straight and tall. She stared after him as he started to move inside the door. He paused, looking in her direction for the briefest of minutes, caught in the light from the house. She realized that he had short, dark hair. His jaw was clean-shaven, his nose like a blade. Everything about him was lean and hard. Except for the expression in his eyes, which was…unreadable. For just a second there, staring at this man who was the epitome of masculinity, something inherently feminine awakened and shivered through her. An unwelcome something. She had had enough of male dominance in her life. What she wanted was a rest, a reprieve before she moved on and made a place for herself and Grace far away from her roots and her past. She didn't want to recognize whatever elemental something in this man that evoked a purely female and involuntary reaction.

And she didn't have to. In just a minute, he and Scrap had disappeared back inside the house. He left the light burning, and she wondered if it was for her sake, or if he'd simply forgotten to turn it off. Probably forgotten. The light didn't quite reach the car, anyway.

Quickly she fed her baby, cuddled her close for a few minutes, then put her back into her car seat to sleep. The dark and the stress of the day overtook her, and Susanna felt the world slipping away.

She awoke with a start. Sitting in the cramped car seat, she had fallen half over, and her body jerked her out of sleep. She blinked several times as reality set in and she remembered where she was.

There was still no sign of the tow truck.

But sitting on the hood of the car was a battery-powered lantern, a pillow, two blankets and a box.

Glancing around warily, Susanna realized that it really was just her and Grace and the night out here.

She slid open the door and hauled the things inside.

Flipping open the box, she found a sandwich and a thermos of milk.

"Thank you, Mr. Malone," she whispered, after she had eaten the sandwich and had done her best to make herself comfortable with the blanket and pillow. She tucked the other blanket half over Grace's car seat.

She wondered if her Mr. Malone would come outside when the tow truck arrived so that she could thank him properly and return the things she'd borrowed.

But when she awoke the next time to the sound of an engine beside her car, it was already morning, and the man in the house was nowhere in sight.

Through the shadowlands and beyond...

Three women stand united against an encroaching evil. Each is driven by a personal destiny, yet they share a fierce sense of love, justice and determination to protect what is theirs. Will the spirit and strength of these women be enough to turn back the tide of evil?

On sale May 25.
Visit your local bookseller.

www.LUNA-Books.com

LAK207

COMING NEXT MONTH

#1722 THE BLACK KNIGHT'S BRIDE—
Myrna Mackenzie
The Brides of Red Rose
Susanna Wright figured a town without men was just the place for a love-wary single mom to start over, but then she ended up on former bad boy Brady Malone's doorstep. Despite the fact that Brady's defenses rivaled a medieval knight's armor, he agreed to help the delicate damsel in distress. Now she planned to help this handsome recluse out of his shell—and into her arms!

#1723 BECAUSE OF BABY—Donna Clayton
Soulmates
Once upon a time there was a sexy widower whose precious two-year-old daughter simply wouldn't quiet down. Suddenly a beautiful woman named Fern appeared, but while she calmed his cranky child, she sent *his* heart racing! Paul Roland knew it would take something more magical than a pixie-like nanny to bring romance into his life. But magic didn't exist…did it?

#1724 THE DADDY'S PROMISE—Shirley Jump
Anita Ricardo wanted a family but Mr. Right was nowhere to be found—enter the Do-It-Yourself Sperm Bank. But the pregnant self-starter's happily-ever-after wasn't working out—her house was falling apart, her money was gone and Luke Dole was turning up everywhere! She agreed to tutor the handsome widower's rebellious daughter, but *Luke* was the one teaching her Chemistry 101….

#1725 MAKE ME A MATCH—Alice Sharpe
When Lora Gifford decided to sidetrack her matchmaking mother and grandmother by hooking them up with loves of their own, she never counted on infuriating, heart-stopping, sexy-as-sin veterinarian Jon Woods sidetracking her from her mission. Plan B: Use kisses, caresses—*any means possible!*—to get the stubborn vet to make his temporary stay permanent.

SRCNM0504